ALSO BY
MATT WALLACE

Bump

*The Supervillain's Guide
to Being a Fat Kid*

NOWHERE SPECIAL

MATT WALLACE

KT KATHERINE TEGEN BOOKS
An Imprint of HarperCollins Publishers

Katherine Tegen Books is an imprint of HarperCollins Publishers.

Nowhere Special
Copyright © 2023 by Matt Wallace
195 Broadway, New York, NY 10007.
www.harpercollinschildrens.com

Library of Congress Cataloging-in-Publication Data

Names: Wallace, Matt, 1982– author.
Title: Nowhere special / Matt Wallace.
Description: First edition. | New York : Katherine Tegen Books, an imprint of
HarperCollins Publishers, [2023] | Audience: Ages 8–12. | Audience: Grades 4–6. |
Summary: Twelve-year-old Stan and Elpidia find hope in an unexpected friendship
as they navigate challenging family circumstances and a dangerous
local gang in the desolate Southern California desert.
Identifiers: LCCN 2022058993 | ISBN 9780063254008 (hardcover)
Subjects: CYAC: Friendship—Fiction. | Family problems—Fiction. |
   Child abuse—Fiction. | Bullies and bullying—Fiction. | Gangs—Fiction. |
   City and town life—Fiction. | Mexican Americans—Fiction.
Classification: LCC PZ7.1.W3535 No 2023 | DDC [Fic]—dc23
LC record available at https://lccn.loc.gov/2022058993

23 24 25 26 27 LBC 5 4 3 2 1
First Edition

For all the kids in the desert I left behind.
And for the mentors who taught me how to fight,
in every sense of the word.

A Content Advisory from the Author

This novel contains depictions of domestic violence involving women and children as well as discussions of racially charged topics, in particular racism and colorism. While not actually depicting any of the following, it also contains references to drug addiction, drug use, and the manufacture and sale of illegal drugs.

These are all heavy issues with very personal meanings to me, and I've done my absolute best to write about them in a way that will be appropriate for preteen readers. However, if any of this is subject matter you as a parent, teacher, librarian, or anyone else responsible for a middle-grade-age reader would prefer that reader not be exposed to at this point, I can't in good conscience recommend my story.

I believe it is vitally important we know what media our kids are consuming and that we are also involved in the discussion of that media with them. I want this novel to be a catalyst for that kind of conversation, and I feel the topics addressed in this book are important for kids to learn about, understand, and discuss in a constructive and healthy way. That's why I've written the story I have.

Thank you for taking the time to read this, and I hope it helps you make an informed decision.

—Matt Wallace

1

"Did you know scorpions have six
or seven eyes? But they can't see much,
even with all those eyes. That's like a lot
of people nowadays. The more they have,
the less they see."
—*CHARLIE*

Getting punched in the face for the first time doesn't really feel like anything, at least right away. It's like turning around and bumping into a wall you didn't know was there. You know something knocked into you, but it doesn't *hurt*. A few seconds later, your cheek might start to sting, like getting a mosquito bite, but soon there's this tingle that feels the way soda looks when you pour it into a glass, all fizzing and bubbling. After that, your cheek goes numb, and you don't feel anything at all.

The second punch, *that* one hurts right away. The

second punch, you feel each of the tiny little hard bits of bone that stick out when someone makes a fist. It's like the first hit wakes your brain up to what's happening, and by the time the second hit comes, your brain is yelling at your face, telling your cheek what it's going to feel like to get punched. It almost hurts before that fist even touches your face because you're remembering the hit before.

Hopefully by the third punch, you figure out that you should start moving your face away from the fist coming at it, or at least put up your arms to cover and protect yourself.

Elpidia has learned to cover up after the first punch, and if she sees that one coming, sometimes she can even dodge it. Not that it makes much difference; there is no way to avoid the dozens of punches and kicks that follow, especially when it is three against one.

Elpidia had been heading to her favorite tree with her lunch and her notebook. Abuela made albóndigas, Elpidia's favorite meatball soup, at the bar the day before, and she had leftovers in a thermos for her lunch, so she was excited. She was walking across the wide lot of cracked pavement in back of the old church that served as their schoolhouse.

Elpidia felt the little hairs on the back of her neck stand up before she actually saw the three of them. It used to be that the only kids you had to worry about dodging in the yard were members of Los Cocos, the local gang. The ones who were forced to attend school, when they couldn't ditch or otherwise escape, liked to shake the smaller kids down for whatever money or snacks they had on them. Elpidia had been made to hand over more than a few dollars and at least one bag of her favorite chips before.

The way things were now actually made her miss those days.

Her girl cousins, three of them—all from the reservation—were marching toward her. Elpidia's cousin Marigold was out front, always out front, leading the others, who were younger. She was the oldest of them all, almost fourteen, and as tall as any fifteen-year-old boy in school. Elpidia didn't think she'd ever seen the girl smile, not once.

"Hey!" Marigold shouted at her. "Crunchy Girl!"

They'd been calling her that even before all the trouble between the families started, but it had a lot more hate behind it when they said it now. The name came from when they were making fun of the dry skin on her elbows. Marigold said she looked like a crunchy lizard.

"What did your gramma make you today? We're hungry and we don't got a whole restaurant to make our lunch for us."

Since school began and they started giving her a hard

time, Abuela had told Elpidia half a dozen times to ignore the girls.

Elpidia was never very good at keeping her mouth shut, though.

"I don't got anything for you," she told them, "but I saw a big pile of dog poop in the parking lot if you're hungry like that. It's probably cold by now, but at least there's lots of it."

Elpidia made the mistake of taking her eyes off Marigold, just for a second. She glanced over at her favorite tree, wishing they'd just leave her alone and let her go eat and write in her notebook.

When she looked back, the giant girl's fist was already about an inch from her face.

Her eyes were closed when the second punch came, but she felt it.

She put up her arms to shield herself from further blows. When Elpidia caught sight of the other two girls closing in on either side of her, she tried to keep them back by throwing punches of her own, but they came out less like punches and more like her waving her arms to get someone's attention.

Throwing punches always looks so easy in movies, Elpidia thought. *Why does* everything *always look easier in movies?*

She was a thin and scrawny thing, but her arms were strong from helping Abuela in the kitchen every day. She just didn't know how to make that strength work the way she wanted.

Soon she was being beat on from all sides, and there wasn't anything she could do except cover her head with her arms and sink down to her knees, then onto her side. The fists and feet that kept flying at her actually hurt a lot less than Elpidia tossing and turning on top of the broken and pebble-covered concrete. She could feel the tiny rocks scraping her skin all over.

Why is everything that isn't sand covered in stupid little rocks here? Where do they even come from?

Every school she'd ever seen on TV had grass, thick and green and soft.

That's another *thing movies lie about*, she thought.

Finally, Elpidia stopped feeling herself being kicked and punched, and she was able to just lie still on the hard ground. She was out of breath and could feel the left side of her face swelling up big and beating like a heart. It was difficult to open her left eye all the way, too.

With her right eye, she looked into the bright afternoon sun and saw Mrs. Perrio standing over her. She was an old lump of a woman with a whistle around her neck and a face that was cracked like the clay walls of the school itself.

Mrs. Perrio yelled at Elpidia's cousins to go back inside and stay there until lunch was over.

"Do you need to go to the nurse?" she asked Elpidia.

"Is she even here today?" Elpidia reminded her.

"Get off the ground and go see."

She knew that was as much help as she was going to get from the woman.

Elpidia used to like the schoolyard at lunchtime. She'd sit under one of the dead trees scattered at the edges of the concrete, trying to find as many thin stripes of shade given off by the tree's leafless branches as she could. She'd write down ideas for new recipes in her notebook, or ideas for the food truck she was going to have one day. Elpidia had two pages that were just lists of different names she'd come up with for it, and drawings of how the name would look on the side of the truck.

That all changed when the new year started. Actually, the way Elpidia figured, it changed over the summer before school was back in session, after her mother and father went away. That had been hard enough, but when Abuela threw her big Fourth of July party she did every year and none of their Cahuilla relatives came, the first time that had ever happened, Elpidia knew there were other problems.

Elpidia never really talked or hung out much with her

cousins from the reservation when they were at school. For as long as she could remember, any time they'd played together or laughed together, it had always been at family gatherings. It was like living in two different worlds. Elpidia never knew why it was that way. It probably didn't help that she wasn't great at making friends.

So, for years they'd pretty much ignored each other on the schoolyard. But at least when the two sides of their family were still talking, Marigold had never been mean to her. Not anymore, though. Elpidia never knew how good she'd had it before.

Her backpack had fallen off when Marigold jumped her, and it was open. Everything had spilled out next to the little strips of blood she'd left on the ground. She started scooping everything up and stuffing it back inside her backpack, swallowing and sucking tears and snot and more blood through her nose.

Elpidia panicked when she couldn't find her notebook. She didn't care about the beaten-up schoolbooks, most of them held together with rotting brown tape, but she had to have her recipes and truck ideas. Her dirty, scratched-up hand helplessly searched the ground around her, but there was nothing.

Then, with her good eye, she saw a big, chubby hand holding out her notebook to her.

Elpidia knew the boy's name, but that was about it. It wasn't like she could forget. Stan was the only white kid in her class, and he was the biggest kid by a lot, too.

"Thanks," she mumbled, taking the notebook and slipping it into her backpack.

She saw him open his mouth like he was going to say something, but no words came out.

Elpidia waited for him to figure it out. She waited until it felt really weird and uncomfortable.

Stan still didn't say anything.

She finally zipped up her backpack and shouldered it, walking away from him to the little shack that served as one of the school's only bathrooms. It was set away from the main building, so Elpidia knew her cousins wouldn't be waiting for her there.

You "locked" the door from inside by fastening a string tied to a hook nailed into the wall. Elpidia pulled the string tight, wanting to be alone. There was one toilet, filled with chemicals that smelled just as bad as what people left in there, Elpidia always thought. Whoever had turned the old church into a school had put in a big rubber sink and hung a cracked, filthy mirror above it.

Elpidia dropped her backpack and leaned over the sink, turning on the weak stream of water that dribbled from the tap. It stung when she splashed the water onto her face, especially on the left side, but it felt good, too.

There were no paper towels. There were *never* any paper towels. She wiped down her face with her hands and then rubbed her palms together fast and hard, looking up at her reflection in the mirror.

Her left eye was red and purple and swollen half shut. Her cheek was swollen, too, and it was bleeding. She had a cut on the middle of her bottom lip.

What she saw in the mirror didn't really bother her. If anything, it bothered her *because* it didn't bother her. She should have been mad—at her cousins, at Mrs. Perrio not caring. She should have wanted revenge. She should be crying hot, angry tears into the sink.

Mostly, though, Elpidia just felt tired. This place was so *small*. All the kids bused to the same little school. All their parents working in the same date fields and drinking and eating in the same bar, shopping in the same general store. She knew how big the world was supposed to be. She'd never seen any of it except for here, but she knew it was out there. The desert they all lived in looked big, but it wasn't. It was too small for her to go anywhere, to do anything without the same sad, angry people there to ruin it.

One day, she thought, dabbing at her split lip with a wet fingertip. *When I can learn to drive and get my truck.*

She'd pick a direction and just drive, until she ran out of money, then she'd sell her food until she had enough to keep going, over and over again until she was on the other side of the world.

It didn't really matter which direction, as long as it was away from here.

2

"You'd think the mint would be too much,
that it would make the meatballs too
sweet. But sometimes things that seem
like they don't go together are really the
things that make each other whole."
—ABUELA

The smell from the lake woke Stan up fifteen minutes
before his mom knocked at his bedroom door to get
him out of bed.

Winter was the worst time for that smell because it
was the windiest, and those winds brought the awful odor
of dead fish and salt right to every window and doorway.
Stan's family lived close enough to the lake that Stan could
see the shore from his bedroom. He hated it. He hated
having to walk near it. The ground crunched under your
feet. It felt like walking on old bones.

He sat in front of the little scratched-up writing desk his mom had gotten for him at the secondhand store out on Route 86. He'd started a new story the night before and worked on it until he couldn't keep his eyes open any longer.

He was back to writing by hand in his notebook since his laptop died. His mom had saved up to order him a used one off eBay, and it had been the best thing ever. He'd had it for the whole summer before it just stopped turning on one day. Having to go back to writing with a pen sucked bad enough—Stan wrote so slowly that way—but he also had a bunch of stuff he'd written on the laptop that was stuck in it now until they could afford to get it fixed.

Stan's mom knocked on the door, softly, not wanting to wake up his dad.

"I'm up," he said, barely above a whisper.

"Okay, hon," she whispered back through the door.

Stan stopped writing, closing his notebook and stashing it in his backpack along with his pen. He went to comb his hair into something that looked like he didn't just roll out of bed. He needed a haircut.

He hated all his clothes. Everything was too tight. He hated the way his belly and his chest bulged out in all his shirts. He was grateful for his big, baggy gray-and-black hoodie. He wore it pretty much all year, even during the hottest months of summer when it made him sweat like he was walking through a swimming pool. He picked an old shirt from the one and only time his family had made the three-hour drive to Disneyland, and that was two years ago.

When he walked out into the living room, his dad was asleep on the couch, wearing the same clothes he had on the day before. That was most mornings for as long as Stan could remember. It used to bother Stan, but he'd come to like it this way. Mornings were quiet, peaceful. By the time he got home from school, his dad would be awake and drinking his third beer, and it wouldn't be quiet anymore.

His mom walked up to him, holding a finger over her lips, as if he needed to be reminded to be quiet. She gave him his lunch and a donut for breakfast. It was two days old, and the glaze was weird where it wasn't broken off. He ate it quickly.

It was a long walk to school, but Stan had stopped taking the bus the year before. It started to get so that he got a stomachache just waiting for the bus to come pick him up. It was a zoo inside that thing, and no one, absolutely no one, wanted the fat kid sitting next to them. There was never an open seat by the time the bus got to Stan, and the other kids, whether they were in his own class or older, never wanted to move over for him to sit. It could get ugly, and the names they called him weren't any prettier.

His family only had one car that barely worked most of the time. His dad always fell asleep with the keys in his pocket, and his mom never wanted to wake him up in the morning to try to get them.

Stan walked up the middle of the gravelly roads. There were never any cars this early. Not that there were ever that many cars this far out in the desert. He had an old, faded paperback novel in one of his pockets, and he pulled it out to read as the sun came up over the mountains. The book was called *Under the Moons of Sigma Seven*. It was about a soldier who travels to fight a war on another planet. He always liked stories about people leaving Earth to go live somewhere else.

It was just a few minutes before the start of class when Stan crossed the school parking lot. The school itself was really an old adobe church. It still had a big cross and a bell hanging over the front doors. The whole thing looked like a big clay sculpture any of the kids who went there might have made in art.

He kept his head down and buried inside his hoodie as he walked past the other kids hanging out on the school steps. Sometimes they whispered about him in Spanish. A lot of times they didn't bother to whisper. Other times they said things right to his face. Stan understood a lot more than he let them know he did, but he always felt too embarrassed to try to speak Spanish back to them.

Class was always slow. Their teacher, Mr. Tapia, taught the kids in school who were in grades four through six, and all of them had different lessons and different tasks depending on their level, so he had to take them through everything one grade at a time.

Stan read a lot of books on his own in class.

That day the sixth graders had a math test in the morning and one-page essays due before lunch. Stan bombed the math test because he hated numbers, but he always aced the essays. For this one, they were supposed to write about one of the old Spanish missions they'd been reading about. Stan chose San Juan Capistrano, where swallow birds returned every year around the same time. He'd written it like it was one of the swallows telling a story about why they kept coming back to the mission. Mr. Tapia always liked it when he got creative like that.

At lunchtime he crept around the edge of the yard to where his favorite tree had died years ago but was still standing tall. His mom had given him a cereal bar and a warm soda to take that day, and he was almost to the end of *Under the Moons of Sigma Seven*.

He was halfway through his cereal bar when the fight broke out on the yard. Stan heard the girls yelling before he looked up from the end of his book to see the three older ones circling Elpidia like wolves.

He knew Elpidia from class, but he'd never really talked to her. He'd wanted to, a bunch of times, because at lunch she liked to sit alone under one of the trees like he did. She even liked writing in her notebook like he did, although Stan was pretty sure she wasn't writing stories in hers. He'd walked by her on purpose a few times to try to catch a glimpse at her notebook pages, but it looked like lists of things he couldn't really make out.

It was the third or fourth time he'd seen a fight break out between the group of girls since school started again. Elpidia never did anything that he could see to make them mad. It was always the other three coming up to her. He felt his heart start beating fast as he watched Elpidia crumple up on the ground. He closed his fists tight, until his knuckles turned white. He didn't understand why no one ever helped her, but as much as he wanted to, Stan never did, either.

He didn't know how to fight, and even if he did, what was he going to do? Go over there and start punching a bunch of girls?

Finally, their lunchtime teacher broke it up. Stan waited until Mrs. Perrio went away, and then he got up from his spot against the tree and walked over to where

16

Elpidia was gathering up the stuff that had fallen out of her backpack. The same notebook he'd tried so hard to get a peek inside of had flown across the yard, and he leaned down and picked it up as he walked past.

As he handed it to her, his eyes went wide when he saw how messed up her face was. It made him feel even worse for not doing anything more to help her.

Elpidia thanked him. It was the first thing she'd ever said to him.

He wanted to tell her he was sorry, for what happened, but more that he didn't do anything about it. Stan couldn't seem to find the words, though. He was never good with words when it came to talking to other people. He needed the time and space to write things down.

Elpidia looked at him like he was a giant weird simp, and as soon as she had her notebook zipped inside her backpack again, she shuffled away from him.

Stan couldn't blame her.

3

"There's no mess that can't be
cleaned up. There's just messes people
don't want to clean up."
—*FLAVIO THE BUSBOY*

The room smelled like cough syrup and also like some
kind of food had gone bad inside of it. There were no
windows to open, and Elpidia felt like she was wearing the
air because it was so hot. The heat only made the smells
worse. She sat on the edge of a skinny examination bed
with a strip of crinkly paper down the middle of it. The
bed was made of what felt like plastic, and it was torn in at
least six places that Elpidia could see, with stained bits of
foam spilling out.

The "nurse's office" was more like a big closet someone

had cleaned out. Besides the bed, there was a sink that was either dirty or rusted or both, and a little cabinet they used to keep medicine and other supplies in, but people kept breaking in and stealing all of it. Now the cabinet was mostly empty, just a couple of open boxes of Band-Aid strips and a plastic bin filled with used ChapSticks.

Her cheek felt like it had a heartbeat. Elpidia could feel the blood pumping under her skin there, and some of it had even leaked out. Her bottom lip was double its normal size, and she couldn't really feel any of it.

Her eye was the worst. She could barely see out of it, and all the skin around was hard and swollen, and it tingled like when your arm or leg goes to sleep.

Elpidia was lucky her cousins had picked today to kick her butt. The nurse only came to their school twice a week. She was a retired nurse who volunteered at schools like theirs all around the deserts of Southern California. She was an old white lady, and Elpidia always felt like she treated the kids more like hurt or sick animals than people. Still, hospitals cost money. Drugstores cost money. The nurse fixed you up for free, or at least she fixed you up as best she could.

The old woman didn't smell as bad to Elpidia as the room around them did, but she didn't smell much better, either. Elpidia tried not to show how much it bothered her, but she couldn't do anything about sweating from the heat. The nurse dabbed a wet cotton ball against her cheek, and whatever the wet part was stung worse than getting punched there had. She tried to hold still and not make any noise. Elpidia didn't know why it was so important to her to act brave or tough. Maybe it was because she didn't feel like she'd been either of those things out in the yard with her cousins.

"What did you say to make those girls so angry?" the nurse asked.

"Nothing," Elpidia answered quietly.

"You must've said *something*."

Those words hurt Elpidia worse than the beatdown or the chemicals the nurse was using on her bloodied face. What the nurse said also made Elpidia so angry. The old woman didn't even ask what actually *happened*—she just assumed it had to be Elpidia's fault.

Adults could be so dumb, she thought. They needed everything to make some kind of sense to them, even though most things in the world didn't make any sense. Elpidia had figured that out when she was, like, eight years old. She suspected adults had to do that because if they admitted that the way the world and people are don't make sense, they'd actually have to try to change them. They'd have to ask questions that made them feel confused and afraid and uncomfortable.

Elpidia didn't say any of that to the nurse, of course. Nothing made people like her madder than someone, especially a kid like Elpidia, telling them how wrong they were.

The nurse peeled the paper away from a sticky bandage and carefully fitted it over the cut on Elpidia's cheek she'd just finished cleaning up and treating with the burning medicine.

"Now, that *eye*," the old woman practically groaned, shaking her head as she leaned in to examine the swollen skin making it hard for Elpidia to see.

The nurse fished a little white plastic penlight out of her first-aid kit and clicked one end of it, making the other end light up. The light didn't seem that bright until the nurse shone it right into her injured eye. Even through the swelling, it was painful to look at. Elpidia began to turn away from the light until the nurse snapped at her.

"Hold still now!"

"Take that thing out of my nieta's eye," someone standing behind the nurse ordered her.

It wasn't a loud or deep voice. You could hear the speaker was old, and she sounded tired and small. Still, there was something about that voice you didn't argue with. It didn't matter if you knew Elpidia's grandmother or not, it was like you heard the spirit living inside her tiny, wrinkled body, and that spirit was big enough to swallow you whole if you gave it any trouble.

Her abuela stood just inside the cramped room, leaning on her cane. Just past her seventy-fifth birthday, she was barely as tall as Elpidia was at twelve. Her aunts and uncles assured her that Abuela had shrunk as she'd aged, but Elpidia always remembered her being that short and that old. Nothing about the woman ever changed, really. The same giant market bag always hung from her shoulder. She wore the same black housecoat that came to her knees. She was usually wearing her stained apron under it because she spent so much time in the kitchen of her cantina. She wore dark glasses over her eyes, even inside, because the light hurt them. Elpidia couldn't even remember what color her grandmother's eyes were or how they looked without the shades.

And she always had her cane, a polished and shiny piece of wood from a mesquite tree. Her husband, Elpidia's grandfather, who she'd never gotten to know, had made it for Abuela many years ago before he passed away. The top of the cane was carved to look like a little skull wearing a tall top hat. Her grandmother carried it everywhere, and she carved little notches in it every time she had to whack some out-of-control or nasty bar customer with the wooden stick. There must have been twenty or more of the little markings.

The only place she didn't use it was in the kitchen, while she cooked. It was like being in her kitchen turned back time for Abuela. She didn't feel the aches and pains in her legs and hips and hands when she was making her food. It was one of the reasons Elpidia loved to cook and wanted to be like her grandmother.

Abuela didn't say another word to the nurse as the other woman turned around. At first Elpidia's grandmother just stood there, slipping the bag from her shoulder and holding the strap with both hands wrapped into fists around it, on top of her cane.

The nurse didn't say anything back, either.

She did click the penlight off, though.

"Mrs. Parra?" the nurse asked, even though they'd met before, more than once.

Abuela nodded.

"It's mostly swelling," the nurse told her. "Once it all goes down, her face'll be back to normal. And I don't think her eye itself is damaged. That cut on her cheek, though, that might need stitches. I've cleaned and closed it as best I can with what I have."

Abuela looked up at the stuffy woman who was probably a few years older than she was.

"You can go now," she said.

For a moment the silence in the room felt thicker and

more uncomfortable than the sweltering heat.

"I'll, uh, leave you two alone for a minute," the nurse offered, like she hadn't heard the order she was just given.

Abuela nodded again, politely, as the nurse stepped around her to leave the room.

Elpidia squirmed where she sat, unsure what to say or how to feel. She didn't know if Abuela was angry or disappointed or upset or all those things at the same time.

Her grandmother walked over to the bed where she sat, the bottom of her cane knocking against the floor with each step. She reached up and gently took Elpidia's chin, squinting behind her dark glasses.

The skin of her grandmother's hand felt like paper. There were hard spots from the work she did, and scars from burning herself on pots or the stove, but her touch still managed to be so soft.

"¿Tus primos?" she asked Elpidia, even though Elpidia felt like Abuela already knew the answer.

She nodded without saying anything.

Her grandmother sighed.

They hadn't talked very much about everything going on between the two sides of the family, not after the fire, not even since Elpidia had been living with her abuela for the past six months.

Her grandmother wasn't much of a talker to begin

with. She spoke through her cooking, through the way she fed everyone around her all the time until they felt like they were going to pop. She let what she did speak for her.

When it came to personal things, family matters, Abuela liked talking about it even less than usual. All she'd told Elpidia since her granddaughter had come to live with her was that time healed everything that could be healed.

Elpidia thought she meant all anyone could do when something really bad happened was wait until they forgot about it, or at least until they didn't think about it every second of every day.

That was harder, she thought, when what happened had changed your whole life. Like both of your parents being taken away to some jail a hundred miles upstate.

"You didn't run away," her grandmother said.

It wasn't a question.

Elpidia shook her head.

"You didn't even try."

"No. Should I have?" she asked. "Would you?"

"I don't run so good," Abuela said, even though Elpidia was sure her grandmother knew that's not what Elpidia was asking.

She didn't say anything else for a long while.

Elpidia just waited, knowing her grandmother did

things in her own time. No one rushed her, and if you tried, it never ended well.

Finally, Abuela nodded, like she'd made a big decision about something.

"You need to learn to fight."

Elpidia's good eye blinked in surprise.

"I know where we need to go," her grandmother announced.

"Where?" Elpidia asked.

Abuela smiled.

"El Escorpión" was all she said.

4

"It's never about winning a fight.
It's just about surviving. If you survived
the fight, you won."
—CHARLIE

Stan was halfway down the block from his house when he heard the first glass shattering.

He'd been reading and walking at the same time, which he liked because it made the walk to and from school go faster. He'd just gotten to the part in the story where the crew of the starship *Rainier* had returned to their home planet to find that somehow they'd traveled six hundred years into the past, and everyone was wearing armor and riding horses and mistook the crew for evil witches. Stan was pumped for a bunch of good laser guns versus sword fights.

The sound of glass breaking violently echoed through the empty street and snapped him out of the reading trance he'd been in.

Then he heard a woman scream, and he knew right away it was his mom.

Stan started running, as fast as he could.

He could barely feel his body as it moved him along. His brain was racing and bubbling, and the rest of him felt cold and shaky. By the time Stan reached their house, he wasn't breathing so much as trying to swallow as much air as he could, and he was already sweating. Still, as he neared the front door, he stopped. He was thinking instead of just reacting now, his brain taking over from his body.

With his brain in charge again, there was fear. He was afraid of what was waiting inside, even if part of him already knew exactly what he was going to see because he'd seen whatever it was before. That fear slowed him down. That fear made him reach out to open the door with a shaking hand that took as long as it could to grab the doorknob.

Stan had to open the door, though. There'd been times before when he'd run away from the noises instead of toward them, and that always felt worse later.

He could see the opening into the kitchen when he walked through the front door. A chair from the table in there was lying on its side on the floor, and Stan could see pieces of a broken, food-stained plate. He didn't know if someone had dropped it or thrown it across the room. He'd seen both happen before. He'd seen his father throw things in anger, and he'd seen his mom throw things to try to protect herself and him from all that anger.

His legs felt numb from running. The rest of how he felt, shaking and cold and weak, was from how nervous he was.

"Mom!" Stan yelled as he stumbled into the kitchen, almost tripping over his own feet.

His father was holding her by both arms, pushing the top half of her body over the kitchen counter so she couldn't get away. There were more broken plates and cups at their feet, some with food sticking to them.

Stan didn't know what to do. He wasn't out of breath from running anymore, but he could still barely breathe from the fear.

His father hadn't even turned his head, but Stan's mom saw him standing there as she continued to struggle against the man who was almost twice her size.

"Honey, go to your room!" his mom called to him.

She was trying to sound calm, but it just made her voice even scarier to listen to.

"Stop it!" Stan yelled at his father's back.

Stan ran across the kitchen. He grabbed his father by the belt and pulled as hard as he could, trying and failing to drag him away from his mom. His father was a big man, and Stan wasn't strong enough to move him on his own, or even with his mom pushing from the other side, but that didn't stop him from trying, refusing to let go even though it wasn't working.

His father finally became aware Stan was in the room. He turned his head just long enough to see who it was tugging at him before his father swung an arm into the side of Stan's head and knocked him back into the refrigerator.

Stan hit the refrigerator door so hard it popped open, and his body bounced off it and fell to the floor. There was a loud ringing in his ear, the one that had taken most of the swing, and it stung painfully. There was a weird feeling in his head, too, like someone had stuffed it full of cotton. He was having trouble seeing straight. There was two of everything, and the room was spinning around him.

Stan got to his knees, blinking until everything stopped moving again, and then slowly pushed himself up until he could get his feet under himself.

The first thing he saw when he stood was a red, drunken face staring down at him.

His father had turned around, away from the counter. He seemed to have forgotten all about Stan's mom. He was looking at Stan now, breathing as hard and as fast as Stan was.

"What was that?" his father asked, the words barely sounding like words because he'd been drinking.

Stan thought his father was angry, but then he started laughing. He was laughing at Stan. It was a terrible sound. There was nothing happy or fun about it, and it made spit fly over the man's lips.

"You pullin' on me like a little girl?" his father asked as he wiped his chin with the sleeve of his dirty shirt. "You wanna do somethin'? Why don't you throw hands like a man? Huh?!"

He'd stopped laughing. Now there was anger, in his voice and in his eyes. He looked at Stan like he was something gross he'd just found on the bottom of his shoe.

At least he'd let go of Stan's mom. She slipped from between his body and the counter and moved to the other side of the kitchen, holding the edge of the counter as she went like she didn't trust her legs to hold her up.

"You ever even thrown a punch before?" his father pressed Stan. "You haven't, have you? You been beat up though, right? And you never did nothin' back, I bet. Probably just . . . curled up into a big ol' ball on the ground. You fat little coward."

"Bill, leave him alone," Stan's mom said quietly.

"You *shut your mouth*!"

His father's voice was like thunder. It made Stan jump.

"All right, c'mon," his father said, motioning at Stan with his hands to come at him.

Stan still didn't move.

"I'll make it easy for you, okay?"

His father walked a step closer and then dropped down to both of his knees there on the hard surface of their kitchen floor. It must've hurt, but he was too drunk to really feel it or anything else, Stan figured.

Their eyes were on the same level now. Stan's were wide and wet. His father's were red as blood and filled with what looked to Stan like every bad feeling a person could have.

"C'mon," his father demanded, "show me somethin'!"

His breath smelled like a garbage dump. It was so foul, it made Stan's eyes sting and fill with more tears. He turned his head just to get away from the stink of it.

"Stop this, *please*!" his mom begged. "You're scaring him!"

"He's always scared!" Stan's father yelled back without taking his eyes off his son.

His father grabbed him by the chin, hard, and jerked Stan's face back toward his. A sharp pain shot through the back of Stan's neck. He felt the small muscles there get tight and hot.

"You show me you can be a man," his father ordered him.

When Stan still didn't say or do anything, two big, strong hands pushed him, slamming hard into his chest and shoulders. Stan stumbled back a step and almost fell.

"Show me, I said!" his father demanded.

Stan's arms had been hanging at his sides the whole time. He balled both hands into fists against his hips, felt the skin stretch and pull over his knuckles, felt his nails, which were a little too long, dig into the meat of the inside of his hands until it hurt.

He thought about how much his ear hurt. He thought about all the times his father's aim had been better. Stan thought about the bruises that had taken weeks to finally go away. He thought about how his mom was always scared, always tiptoeing around the house trying to be quiet, to be invisible. He hated that even more than getting hit.

Stan could see himself, in his head, throwing the fists his father was asking for. The thought felt good. It made all the fear and nerves and pain fade into the background. Thinking about punching his father in the face made Stan feel better than he had felt inside this house in a long time. Standing in the kitchen with broken glass all over the floor, listening to his mother try not to cry, Stan imagined knocking his father out cold, and just pretending in his own mind was enough to make everything seem okay.

But thinking was one thing, and doing was another.

Nothing was okay, not really, and Stan beating up anyone, especially his father, was just a fantasy, like the books he read.

"Pathetic," his father said under his rotten breath.

He didn't sound angry or disgusted anymore; he just sounded tired.

Stan watched as his father raised himself up from the kitchen floor, slowly, the sound of his bones creaking and cracking loud enough to fill the kitchen.

He staggered past Stan like he wasn't even there.

A few seconds later, he heard his father's body fall into its favorite spot on the couch in the living room.

When he was out of sight, Stan's mom came over to him and hugged him with shaking arms.

"It's okay," she whispered in his ringing ear. "It's over now."

Except it wasn't, Stan knew.

He didn't want to cry. He didn't want to prove his father even more right than he already had. He didn't want to make his mom feel worse, either.

They'd pick up all the broken glass, and they'd clean the floor, and they'd pretend it never happened, until it happened again.

5

"The world ends out here,
even if the desert keeps going."
—*MEZCO*

Charlie's place was in the deep desert, far past where the roads stopped being actual streets and became just strips of sand smoothed down by enough cars driving over them for so many years. Everything was flat and dead, and even the mountains in the distance looked more like little hills, and there was nothing green growing on any of them. There were no houses. You might drive past a crumbling shack that had either been burned out by fire or just fell apart because it was so old, but there were no neighborhoods or businesses out this far.

Abuela's old car had no air-conditioning, which meant they had to keep all the windows rolled down. It saved them from melting in the heat, but it also let in the giant cloud of dust that was following them every inch of the way across the desert. The car belonged to Abuela, but she never drove it. She had to give up driving years ago when her eyesight began to fail her. She sat in the back seat with Elpidia, both of her small hands holding the end of her walking cane.

Elpidia's tío Raymond was behind the wheel. He was her uncle, but he wasn't that much older than her, and she thought of him more like a cousin. He'd only been out of school for a few years. Abuela used to have her oldest son, Elpidia's tío Enoc, drive her around everywhere, but he'd gotten a job up north in Los Angeles, and then the year before he'd been arrested, and the US government was trying to deport him back to Mexico. Abuela was still fighting with them to get him back. They visited him in this place down by the border that looked like a business building but that they all treated like it was a prison. It was the first time Elpidia had the thought that jail could be someplace without any cages or bars.

The three of them had been sweating and choking on dust inside the car for almost forty minutes, at least. Abuela still hadn't told her where they were going, but

Elpidia thought she'd figured it out a while ago, or at least she had a pretty good guess. There was only one person she knew of who lived out this far from Lakeshore Estates the wrong way into the desert.

Elpidia had never met Charlie Ramos, but she'd heard about him. Most of the kids at school had. He drove out from his place every now and then and crossed the train tracks to buy food and other supplies at Poor Richard's, the store down the road from Abuela's bar, and the only place in Lakeshore Estates to buy any kind of groceries. One time a few years ago, he'd gotten in a fight in the parking lot with a bunch of bros from up north who were driving their dirt bikes out to the dunes. How many of them there were depended on who was telling the story. Elpidia had heard Charlie fought three guys, and she'd also heard there were ten of them.

However many there were, Charlie Ramos had dropped them all. People who told the story talked about the fight, especially the ones who claimed to have seen it themselves, like it was something out of a John Wick movie.

Since then there were all kinds of stories about Charlie. Some people said he'd been a Special Forces soldier in the army. Other people said he used to be in a rock band in the Philippines. Some people even said he was Manny Pacquiao's cousin and had taught Manny how to box.

Nobody really knew, though. Nobody hung out with him, or had ever even talked to him, as far as Elpidia could tell. He was kind of the Obi-Wan Kenobi of Lakeshore Estates.

It was another twenty minutes before Elpidia started seeing a bunch of dots in the desert far ahead of them. As they drove closer, the dots became buildings, three of them, and a few different trucks and cars. There was what Elpidia guessed was supposed to be a house, or at least it was the biggest building of the three. It looked more like four or five different small shacks bolted together. The "roof" (it looked like there was more than one) was half a dozen different kinds and colors of metal. Some of the walls were wood and some were cement blocks. There were dark plastic trash bags over most of the windows.

On the largest wall, somebody had painted a big yellow sun with eight rays shooting out all around it.

Far off from the main house, there was what looked like a garage. The front was open and the inside was dark, but you could make out the rear ends of a couple of old cars inside it.

The smallest building was like a lot of the shacks they'd seen while driving through the deep desert, except this one hadn't fallen apart yet. It was tall with a slanted roof and one skinny little door. There were no windows, but Elpidia could see a long pipe rising out through the top of the crooked roof, like something you'd see on a factory.

All around the little patch of desert Charlie apparently called his home, there was a barbed-wire fence protecting what little he had. The wire was strung between wood posts struck into the ground. Every post was a different height and shape, like branches broken from a giant tree. Tío Raymond drove through the only opening in the fence, which was just big enough for their car to fit. As they passed through the gate, Elpidia saw that each of the posts on either side of them was decorated with what looked like the shells of armadillos tied to them.

"This place is spooky, yo," Raymond said as he pulled up in front of the main house and put the car in park.

"You act like you grew up in a palace," Abuela chastised him, already flinging her door open and sticking her cane out into the sand.

They climbed out of the car, Elpidia last. She wasn't *scared*, not really, not with Abuela and Tío Raymond there beside her.

She was nervous, though. Like it was the first day of school or something.

In a way, she guessed it was.

"Should I go knock?" Raymond asked Abuela.

Before she could answer, they all heard the rusty hinges of the door creaking.

Elpidia had been looking at the old cars and trucks. There must have been half a dozen of them, and none of them looked like they worked. Most didn't even have wheels.

She turned just in time to see a lanky figure duck under the doorway to walk outside of the house.

Charlie Ramos was as tall and skinny as the crooked fence posts that surrounded his home. His hair was long and dark with threads of silver. It was thick and big on top of his head. Elpidia thought it almost looked like a wig.

His face looked different than any other Elpidia had seen up close before. He had a thin mustache the same color as his hair with the same bits of gray in it. And there were scars. He had a bunch of little ones, all in different places, one across his right cheek, another through his left eyebrow, and a couple curving around the bottom of his chin.

Even though she found his face interesting, she couldn't stop looking at the belt holding up his ripped and faded blue jeans. It was brown cracked leather, but what kept catching her eye was the buckle. Charlie's belt buckle was huge, big enough to use as a plate, with what looked like plastic or glass over the front of it. Under that clear cover,

Elpidia knew she was looking at what used to be a living scorpion. There was no doubt in her head that it was real. It wasn't alive anymore; someone had preserved it perfectly and spread out its tail and claws to show it off.

El Escorpión, she remembered her grandmother saying.

How did Abuela know Charlie Ramos, Elpidia wondered.

Then she noticed the knife clipped to Charlie's belt, just above his hip. Most of the men in Elpidia's family carried folding knives in covered holsters on their belts; Abuela carried one in her market bag.

Elpidia had never seen a knife like this, though. It was smaller, with a short blade that curved into almost a half circle. It made her think of a claw, like on the raptors in those dinosaur movies. On the other end of the knife, attached to the handle, was a metal ring, almost like you'd wear around your finger.

Charlie didn't say anything as he walked up to the three of them. He moved strangely, Elpidia thought. His long legs bent like bows every time he took a step, and he was so *quiet*. You couldn't even hear him walking across the sand.

Abuela dug into what always seemed to Elpidia like the bottomless space inside her bag. She pulled out a wad of bills; Elpidia couldn't tell how much money it was.

The old woman had to reach up to offer it to Charlie. She was barely taller than his waist.

Charlie took the money, still without saying anything. He didn't count it. He barely even looked at it, just tucked it into the front pocket of his old ripped-up jeans.

He was looking at Elpidia the whole time. It made her even more nervous; again, she wasn't scared, but she didn't know what she was supposed to do.

Also, Charlie didn't scare her. She wasn't sure why.

He took a few steps toward her. His vaquero boots still didn't make a sound.

Charlie bent down and rested one knee against the sand. He still had to hunch over a bit in order to be eye to eye with Elpidia.

She felt like he was sizing her up or something. The way you did before you picked someone for your team.

Slowly, a smile spread across his lips. Charlie reached up and extended one of his thin, rough hands to her, like he was offering her a handshake.

Something in his smile reminded Elpidia of her father, or at least her father the way he'd been before, when she was very little, back when she would have trusted him to climb a mountain with her on his back if he wanted.

Elpidia didn't feel nervous anymore. She gripped Charlie's hand with hers and shook it.

"Stronger than you look," he remarked, like he was surprised.

"You too," Elpidia said without thinking.

She shut her lips tight, worried she'd said something wrong, or that he'd take it as an insult.

But Charlie just laughed. His laugh matched his smile.

"Surprise is good," he said. "Surprise is one of your best weapons."

"What are the other ones?" Elpidia asked. "The best weapons?"

Charlie cocked his head to one side, looking at her strangely, but still with that smile on his lips.

He glanced over at her grandmother, who shrugged back at him, as if he'd asked her some silent question.

"That's a good question," Charlie said. "I can see why your lola brought you here."

Elpidia wasn't sure what that meant, but she felt like it might even be a compliment.

Charlie slapped his hands against his knees and stood back up to his full, towering height, looking down on her with something almost like a twinkle in his eye.

"Okay, then," he said. "Let's get started."

6

"At the beginning of a journey
you can be afraid to take the first step,
then by the end of the journey
you don't want to stop walking."
—*MAJOR JAXSON MERCER,*
UNDER THE MOONS OF SIGMA SEVEN

Stan's father wouldn't let his mom have her own car, no matter how many times she made a case for needing one, but he had to let her use his old pickup truck three days a week to go work part-time in the office of a huge date farm about thirty miles from the Salton Sea. Somebody had to bring money into their house to keep them fed and clothed, after all. Besides, Stan's father barely ever went outside anymore, let alone drove the car himself unless it was to the store to buy more beer.

So Stan's mom just told him she'd picked up another

day of work on a Saturday, and she was taking Stan with her. Stan's father didn't seem to care much about either piece of news, but at least he didn't argue with her about any of it. He had his drink and his TV, and he was already half asleep when they left.

"Are you sure about this?" Stan asked as he watched his mom clean out the seats and floor of the truck.

"It's the best I can do, Stan," she said kindly, tossing empty beer cans and old take-out food containers into a trash bag she'd brought outside with them.

"The nearest place that's an actual-type school that I could find is in Indio, and it's too expensive. The YMCA has free lessons, but it's all the way in Palm Desert, and we'd never be able to get you there and back every week. We're lucky there's someone out here who is willing to work with me. With us."

Stan was already regretting saying what he'd said to her. It had been the day after everything that happened in their kitchen with the broken glass and Stan's father trying to push Stan into taking a swing at him. Mom was helping him go over his homework in his bedroom, just before bedtime.

"I want to learn to fight," Stan told her.

He'd surprised and worried her. He could see it all over her face.

45

"What are you talking about?"

"Like, learn martial arts or something? Take classes?"

His mother had sighed like talking about this was going to make her ten years older in the next few minutes.

"Stan, if this is about your dad, you know you can't fight him like that. You were right not to try."

"It's not about that," Stan promised her, even though that wasn't totally the truth. "I'm just . . . scared all the time. You know? I always have been. And I'm tired of it. I'm tired of being scared. I feel like if I knew how to fight, I wouldn't feel like that all the time. I'm not even saying I want to fight anyone, I just . . . I think knowing *how* would be enough. It would help. Maybe."

His mom's mood seemed to change when he said that to her. She looked less tired and worried, and more sad and concerned.

"I understand," she said.

She'd kissed the top of his head and whispered, "I'll see what we can do, okay?"

That was a week ago, and now they were climbing into the newly cleaned-out truck to drive into the desert.

Everything he'd said to his mother was true, but what he didn't tell her was the reason he was saying it now. His father had never challenged Stan before like he had in the kitchen. Until that moment, Stan had never thought about the possibility of fighting back. He'd thought about fighting, sure, but in the same fantasy way he made up his stories. The idea of actually fighting his dad had always seemed as impossible to him as the idea of climbing a mountain.

But even though Stan had frozen in the kitchen when his father taunted and pushed him, there was something in the back of his brain that whispered to him that night. It told Stan he would only keep growing. A day would come soon when he was even bigger than his dad. And if on that day he knew how to fight, things would be a lot different.

Of course, when he'd told his mom he wanted to learn how to fight, Stan meant like in a karate class or something, maybe even some kind of boxing gym. Instead, his mom told Stan about a man she'd met when he did some day work at the farm the year before. She said this guy, Charlie, gave private lessons sometimes.

"Lessons in *what*?" Stan had asked.

"Some kind of fighting. I don't remember the name. I'm pretty sure it's a kind of fighting they do where he's from. He's Filipino. From the Philippines. They're these islands across the ocean."

"I know what they are."

"You do?" his mom asked, surprised.

"No," Stan had admitted.

Stan didn't say much else for the rest of the drive, not until Charlie's compound started to grow large in the distance, and Stan could make out the barbed wire and twisted, armadillo-decorated fence posts.

"This place looks like somewhere a cult would live," Stan said with alarm.

His mom just laughed. "There's no cult here, hon. Charlie is just a nice man who moved out here to be alone. Your dad did the same thing, once upon a time. How do you think we ended up living by the sea like we do?"

"I wish he'd stayed by himself," Stan grumbled, just loud enough for his mom to hear, but she ignored it.

As she drove through the gate, Stan spotted a dark-haired figure who looked like they were jumping around excitedly. At first he thought it might be this Charlie guy himself, but as their truck rolled up to the house, Stan saw it was another kid around his age.

"Does Charlie have kids?" he asked his mom.

"I don't think so."

"I thought you said he gave *private* lessons?" Stan asked.

"I guess he has another student right now. That'll help though, right? You'll have someone to practice and learn with!"

Stan wasn't so sure. Even though he'd thought about taking a class, the one part he'd liked about this idea of his mom's was not having to be around other kids. There'd be no one to make fun of him like when they did sports or outdoor activities at school. What if this new teacher wanted them to run laps together? Stan didn't like running, not just because it made him out of breath or because it made his legs burn and his stomach hurt, but because he always felt embarrassed when he ran. He felt like running made him look stupid, made his belly and other parts of him jiggle through his clothes. He felt slow and uncomfortable.

They both got out of the truck, and his mom went to knock on Charlie's front door.

When Stan recognized Elpidia, he didn't know if he felt better or worse about the situation.

Someone had drawn a pattern in the sand that was either a diamond shape with a line across the middle or two triangles. Stan guessed it counted as both.

Either way, he watched as Elpidia moved around the pattern, turning her body and sweeping her legs so that her steps followed the lines of the triangles. It almost looked like a dance to Stan.

She was good at it, whatever it was, or at least he thought so. She was fast and smooth in her movements and didn't trip over her own feet.

"Good afternoon, Mr. Ramos," said his mom, greeting the tall, lanky man with the messy black and gray hair who answered the door.

"Charlie, magandang babae, Charlie," he said with a smile.

Stan didn't know what the words that weren't "Charlie" meant, but he figured they were a compliment.

"Charlie," his mom repeated, smiling back at the man.

By now Elpidia had stopped what she was doing. She stared across the sand at them all, her eyes moving from Charlie to Stan's mom to Stan himself.

Should I wave at her? Stan wondered. *Will she even remember me?*

He didn't wave.

"And you're sure you're okay with starting now and me paying you next week?" his mom was asking Charlie.

"Sure, sure. I trust your face."

Stan's mom laughed, a little too hard, Stan thought.

"Charlie, this is my son, Stanley," she introduced him.

Stan turned from looking in Elpidia's direction and stared up at Charlie nervously.

"Stan," he said in a quiet voice.

Charlie took a step toward him and crouched down just enough to look Stan in the eyes.

"I bet you're probably tired of hearing you're big for your age," Charlie said a moment later.

Stan nodded. He really did hate hearing about that all the time.

"It's good for what we're going to do, though," Charlie

went on. "You're strong, tall, long arms, big reach. All of that is good."

Stan had never heard *that* before, however. It actually felt kind of good to hear someone describe him as something other than "big" or "husky" or "fat." No one ever seemed to notice anything else about him. Even he'd never thought about his arms having a long reach. He wondered how that was going to help.

"What kind of fighting do you do?" he asked.

Charlie grinned. "It has a lot of names. Escrima, arnis, kali. Really though it's just a way Filipino people figured out how to survive. All through history, people don't seem to like us very much. Probably because we're so good-looking."

Stan's mom laughed at that, too.

Stan didn't laugh, but he did find himself smiling and feeling a lot less nervous talking to Charlie.

"What's . . . what's the way?" he asked. "That Filipino people figured out?"

Charlie shrugged. "You use what you got. Stick, hands. You learn to defend and attack at the same time. You learn how to move to avoid danger. You'll see."

He leaned to one side to look over Stan's shoulder.

"Elpidia!" Charlie called to the girl. "You got someone to spar with now! It's gonna save my knees a lot of pain. Come on over here and say hello."

Stan was suddenly nervous all over again. He turned

just as Elpidia came jogging up to them.

She looked tired from the training they'd been doing, and he could see sweat on her face.

"Hey, Stan," she said. "Weird seeing you here."

Just hearing her say his name threw him off. Even though they'd almost had an actual conversation in the schoolyard the other day, and even though they were in the same class.

"My mom," he started to say, and then stopped himself. "I wanted . . . to learn . . . I mean, I need to know how to . . ."

He felt like the biggest dork in the world.

Elpidia didn't seem to notice, though. She just nodded at him like he had actually said a real, full sentence.

"Me too. At least that's what my grandmother said."

"You ready to get started?" Charlie asked him.

Stan nodded.

To Elpidia, Charlie said, "You want to help me teach him some of the drills we've been doing?"

"Sweet!" Elpidia said with a smile. "I'm graduating to teacher already."

Man, she's cool, Stan thought.

That's when he decided this was, in fact, a good thing.

Maybe the best thing that had happened to him in just about forever.

7

"No sticks, poles, pipes, bats, or similar
objects permitted past this point."
—*U.S. IMMIGRATION AND CUSTOMS
ENFORCEMENT*

"It looks more like a big hotel than a jail," Elpidia
observed as they got closer to the detention center
where her uncle Enoc was being kept.

"Any place you can't leave when you want is a jail,"
Raymond said, sounding mad, but also nervous, like he
wanted to be anywhere else besides here. "Doesn't matter
what it looks like."

"I was just saying, dang," she mumbled from the back
seat, where she sat beside Abuela.

Raymond was behind the wheel, as usual, and her

cousin Ramona was in the front seat next to him. The girl was a lot older than Elpidia, almost eighteen, and she'd been out of school since last year. They weren't close. Besides being older, Ramona always seemed to Elpidia like she thought she was too cool to pay attention to her younger cousins. Raymond called her "trendy," and he didn't mean it as a compliment.

She talked about TikTok a lot.

Like, a *lot*.

Ramona hadn't said much that afternoon, to any of them. She'd spent most of the drive looking at her phone. Elpidia wondered if she was just nervous, too, since it was her father they were all on their way to visit. Her mom and her brothers were in the car following them.

Tío Enoc had been held inside the facility for almost two months. Officers from the Immigration Department raided the warehouse where he was working, and they'd taken everyone away. Her uncle wasn't born in America, but he'd been living and working there every day for longer than Elpidia had been alive. That didn't seem to matter to anyone in charge.

Abuela had hired a lawyer, and they were trying to get the Immigration people to let her uncle go instead of sending him back to Mexico, but from what Elpidia overheard when her grandmother was on the phone with her lawyer, it didn't seem like it was going so well.

Elpidia didn't like long drives, but she did love looking at everything that passed by outside the window. Even if they spent most of the time on the freeway where there wasn't much to see except other cars, cement, and bill-boards, at least it was all new. She could see towns and even cities off in the distance, tall buildings of glass and steel, and all kinds of signs for restaurants and stores they didn't have in the desert.

It was worth the drive to her just to leave the sand behind for a while.

Tío Raymond turned their car onto a long driveway leading to a tall group of buildings that all seemed glued together. Like she'd told him, it looked more like a big, fancy hotel than a prison.

They passed an orange-and-white-striped wooden stand like you'd see when they were doing construction somewhere, to warn people to stay away. There was no construction going on here, though. Instead there was a big piece of poster board taped to the warning stand, a notice posted for visitors. The printing on it said if you were carrying a "sign, banner, or flag," whatever your sign was attached to needed to be made of wood and couldn't be longer than forty inches long.

"Why would people be bringing flags here?" Elpidia

asked, confused by the notice.

"That was probably from a protest they had here," Abuela answered.

"Protest?"

"The families and friends of the people being kept here," her grandmother explained. "Our people, come to say, 'Let everyone go.'"

"Oh. Why weren't we at the protest?"

"Your tío wasn't here then," Raymond said, sounding even more annoyed than before.

That wasn't exactly what Elpidia meant, but she decided not to press it any further.

The parking lot outside the detention center was big and mostly full. Elpidia wondered just exactly how many people they had inside there, and how many of them were like Enoc, just working people who got swept up for what felt to her like no reason.

Raymond found a parking spot not too far from what looked like the main entrance to the massive place. The other car in their little caravan had to keep looking.

Elpidia was the first one to spot the old man climbing onto a big gray-and-black motorcycle a few yards away from them, or at least she was the first one to recognize him and say something.

"Is that . . . Grandpa Jamie?" she asked, surprise and

excitement rising through her voice.

"No way," Raymond said.

"That is *totally* him!" Elpidia insisted.

He was impossible to mistake for anybody else. Her grandfather was the only old Native dude with long white hair she'd ever seen riding around on a motorcycle.

They all got out of the car, Abuela taking her time and using her cane. She wasn't saying anything, which Elpidia thought was weird. Not so much her being quiet, but that Abuela didn't seem surprised.

"Grandpa!" Elpidia called out to him.

When he looked over and smiled at her from the seat of the motorcycle, there was no doubt it was him.

"Little Squirrel!" he hollered back.

It was his private nickname for her, ever since she was four years old and always trying to climb up trees and over tall rocks. Elpidia ran across the cracked pavement and practically jumped up on top of the bike to hug him.

"My granddaughter!" he said as he hugged her back. "You sprouted up a whole inch!"

Her grandfather's face was like the side of a mountain, hard and cracked and faded by the sun. He wore a black leather vest with all kinds of ribbons and buttons and patches on it, some of them funny little sayings, others from motorcycle contests he'd won, and patches from bike clubs to which he'd belonged over the years. Elpidia loved the rings and bracelets he wore, all polished stones and leather bands.

She couldn't remember the last time she'd seen him. Jamie used to hang around the cantina all the time, but since the fire, Elpidia didn't think he'd stopped by once.

"Hola, senorita," he greeted Elpidia's grandmother, saying the "H" in the word "hola" the way she'd expect a white person to do.

"Míyaxwe, James," Abuela said back.

Elpidia recognized the word. It sounded like "mee-yakh-weh." It was Cahuilla for "hello."

"Your Cahuilla is still better than my Espanola," Jamie said with a smile, messing up the word for Spanish even worse than he messed up his greeting.

Even though he was joking around, Elpidia noticed that her grandpa's smile seemed sad.

"It's the only word I remember," Abuela told him.

Grandpa Jamie laughed. "I know that ain't true. You don't forget nothing."

"No, I don't," Abuela said, sounding more serious now.

That seemed to take some of the old man's smile away.

"You still riding that thing, huh?" Abuela asked, staring at Grandpa Jamie's motorcycle.

He nodded. "Until they carry me out boots first."

"What're you doing here?" Raymond asked.

He'd been slow to walk over from the car and join them, hanging back like he might not bother.

"Raymundo!" Grandpa Jamie greeted him happily. "Geez, all of you look like you've grown up on me."

"I stopped growing a long time ago," Raymond told him before repeating, "So what're you doing here?"

Jamie shrugged. "I been coming up most weekends to support Enoc. He's still one of my boys, far as I'm concerned."

Elpidia didn't know that. None of them did, she was pretty sure. But it didn't surprise her. Enoc is one of her mom's brothers, but she knew they'd always been really close, all of Elpidia's uncles on her mom's side and Grandpa Jamie. They'd been friends with her dad before Elpidia's parents were even married. After Abuela's husband died, Jamie kind of became like a father to all of them.

Raymond was too young to remember most of that. She figured that's why it was easy for Raymond to be mad at Grandpa Jamie, even though the one he was really mad at, the one everyone on Abuela's side of the family was mad at, was Elpidia's dad. They all wanted to believe Elpidia's mom was this perfect person, and it was Elpidia's dad's fault she got hooked on the drinking and the pills and whatever else they were doing.

Elpidia seemed to be the only one who knew it wasn't that simple, but no one ever listened to her.

Grandpa Jamie leaned over the handlebars of his motorcycle, peering down at Elpidia and smiling. This time there wasn't as much sadness in it, she didn't think.

"You need to come around more, Little Squirrel. There's barely any rez left in you. You got to keep some of that in your heart. It's part of you, too."

Elpidia started thinking there was a lot she didn't know about her dad's people. Her grandfather was right about that. Living in Lakeshore Estates, away from her relatives on the reservation, always around her mom's family, it was mostly their history and ways she was taught.

For the first time, that made her feel sad.

"She has school, and then she helps me in the cantina," Abuela told him.

Grandpa Jamie sighed. He took a pair of riding gloves from out of the back pocket of his dusty, faded jeans and began to fit them over his hands.

"So much anger between your kinfolk and mine, still. I feel like something that could have brought us all together just sent us even further apart."

"I can't tell anyone how to feel," Abuela said.

For the first time, she sounded like she was upset. It surprised Elpidia. It was as much emotion in the old woman's voice as she ever heard from her grandmother.

"You can still tell them what to do though, right?" Grandpa Jamie pointed out. "We're the elders. It has to be up to us. I don't blame you for anything, Florentina."

He was the only one Elpidia ever heard call Abuela by her first name. It almost sounded to her like he was talking about somebody else.

"It's good to see you," he said, moving his sharp eyes from one face to the next. "All of you. I mean it."

He flashed Elpidia one last smile. Grandpa Jamie fired up the engine of the motorcycle, and it was so loud, Elpidia stuck her fingers in her ears.

She still thought it was cool, though.

She watched him ride away, steering his bike onto that long drive winding from the detention center, and then really revving that thundering engine until he was going so fast, he became a blur.

Elpidia felt a lump forming in her throat.

"C'mon, mija," her grandmother urged her. "Tío's waiting."

"Why didn't Tío Enoc say Grandpa Jamie was coming to visit him this whole time?" Elpidia asked as they all walked to the entrance.

"I don't know, mija," Abuela claimed. "Ask him if you want."

Elpidia wouldn't, though. She was starting to figure out that was the problem, all of them not saying what they were thinking and not talking about what was really going on.

8

"A little blood is good."
—CHARLIE

Stan spent his first couple of Saturdays at Charlie's place catching up to where Elpidia was in her training. Charlie said it was important so they could "spar" together, which was like pretending to fight each other and practicing the moves he taught them.

"He's way too big for me to fight," Elpidia had complained.

Stan was used to people talking about him like that, but it still stung.

He guessed Elpidia could see by the expression on his

face how her words had made him feel because she frowned at him like she felt bad.

"Sorry, I didn't mean it like that. I just meant you're taller than me."

"It's okay," Stan said, and he meant it.

"It don't matter," Charlie assured her. "Not for this, anyway. You just learning the basics right now."

Charlie used a stick to draw a large circle in the sand. He told them both to stand inside of it, right in the middle, facing each other.

He stepped inside the circle with them.

"In Filipino fighting, you learn to use the stick, the knife, the ax. Even double sticks, double knives, double axes. But all of that, the way you move, the way you strike, it all goes into empty hand, too. That's how we going to start, with empty hands. Like this."

Charlie held up both of his hands in front of him, with his palms open and facing out. His arms were extended farther in front of his body than looked natural to Stan.

"This is how you start. You want your hands like this so they can stop what's coming at you. And you want your arms like this because if you keep 'em too close and too tight, you gonna get hit no matter what happens or what I teach you. You want to keep that distance between your precious bits and whatever mean mother wants to mess up those bits. Got that?"

Stan and Elpidia both nodded.

"Second most important thing is you learn to defend and attack at the same time. Let me show you."

Charlie waved Stan over to him and then bent down to one knee, so they were more even in height.

"Throw a punch," Charlie instructed him. "Right at my pretty face. Don't worry if it's ugly. We work on that."

Stan nodded. He tried to think about how they threw punches in movies. He did his best, shooting his arm out toward Charlie's face instead of taking a big wide swing.

Charlie moved ten times faster than Stan had seen him move since they met, way faster than someone as laid-back as Charlie seemed capable of moving.

Charlie used his left hand to push Stan's incoming wrist away and deflect the punch. At the same time, Charlie's right hand shot out and his fist came within a half inch of Stan's nose and mouth.

Stan just stood there, frozen, his eyes wide and crossed as they looked at Charlie's knuckles.

Elpidia looked surprised, too.

"So, there's that, you can counter and strike," Charlie explained. "Here's another thing you can do. Give it to me again, Stanny."

Charlie put his hands back up and waited for Stan to throw another punch.

Stan's feet shifted in the sand. He balled up his fist and

got ready. This time, he threw the punch a little harder, actually trying to connect with Charlie's head.

Again, Charlie swatted Stan's wrist away with his left hand. This time, though, he didn't use his other hand to punch Stan. Instead, Charlie's right hand chopped lightly against the crook of Stan's elbow. It didn't hurt, but it caused Stan's arm to bend. When it did, Charlie grabbed Stan's arm and twisted it slowly so that Stan was forced to bend over at the waist.

"You can trap his arm," Charlie explained. "You can lock up his shoulder."

"Or *her* shoulder," Elpidia corrected him, annoyed.

Charlie grinned. "Of course. Or *her* shoulder. From there you can break their arm if you need to, or you can just hold 'em until they calm down and decide they don't want to fight no more."

He let Stan go.

Charlie showed them a few other ways to block and do what he called "parrying," which was when he swatted Stan's punch away and struck at the same time. He showed them a few more holds and joint locks, too.

When he thought they were ready, he had them start practicing all of it with each other inside the circle, taking turns throwing punches and defending/attacking at the same time.

Stan was trying the shoulder lock Charlie had done on him. He was careful to go slow, but even going slow, one time he twisted Elpidia's arm so her body spun around like a top, and she lost her balance and fell off her feet onto the sand.

"Watch it!" she snapped at him, standing back up and dusting herself off.

"Sorry," Stan said sheepishly. "I'm not doing it on purpose."

"We gotta teach you to control all that strength you got," Charlie said, watching them with a smile on his face.

Elpidia didn't think it was funny, though. She looked mad. Her eyes narrowed, and her face was all scrunched up.

When it was her turn to parry Stan's punch, she leaned in and elbowed him right in the nose with her other arm. She had to throw the elbow almost like a baseball pitcher throwing the ball, just to reach Stan's face, but she connected.

She connected so good it hurt, a lot.

"Oh, my bad!" Elpidia shouted in surprise, cupping her hands over her mouth.

Stan felt something wet and warm touch his lips.

His nose was bleeding.

"Oh my god," he said, leaning forward so the blood didn't drip on his clothes.

"I'm sorry," Elpidia said.

"A little blood's good," Charlie told them, not sounding concerned. "Reminds you what we doing here is real, even if it's just practice."

"I kinda feel like you did that on purpose," Stan said to Elpidia, pinching his nose between his fingers.

She laughed, and that made him mad.

Until Stan figured out she was laughing because pinching his nose made his voice sound like he was a baby who could talk.

That made Stan laugh, too.

Charlie brought him a faded handkerchief for his nose. He tilted Stan's head back and pressed the old cloth to where the blood was trickling out.

"And we got our first training accident out of the way," Charlie said cheerfully. "It's a good day."

Both Stan and Elpidia laughed at that, too.

"Truce, okay?" Elpidia offered, talking to Stan. "I'm sorry I got mad. I know you weren't throwing me around on purpose."

"Truce," Stan agreed. "You totally elbowed me on purpose, but I forgive you."

That made Elpidia smile.

It was weird, Stan thought, but fighting seemed to be a better way to get to know someone than talking.

After their class was over, Elpidia and Stan found

themselves sitting on the hood of one of many old and broken-looking cars spread out across Charlie's compound. Charlie brought them warm Gatorade from an old cooler that apparently didn't keep anything cool. It didn't seem like Charlie had electricity out here.

The Gatorade tasted gross, as all Gatorade does when it's warm, but both Stan and Elpidia drank it anyway without complaining.

Stan shifted nervously against the hot metal hood under him. "Can I ask you something, Charlie?"

Charlie nodded. "Go ahead."

"Why do you like living all the way out here like this?"

"The price is right," Charlie said with a grin. "And by that I mean it's pretty much free."

Elpidia was curious, too. "Is that the only reason?"

Charlie seemed to think about that for a minute.

"Where I grew up, there were people everywhere, man. In the villages, in the cities, it didn't matter. Every place you go, it's packed so tight. You feel like you're inside a tin can or something. When I was a kid like y'all, there were ten of us in a house half the size of the one I got there."

"So, you like the space?" Elpidia asked.

Charlie nodded. "And the quiet. I wasn't always like that, but after I got out the army . . . it taught me to appreciate the quiet life."

"Was that where you learned how to fight? In the army."

"Nah, I been fighting my whole life. Army just pays you for it. Not that the pay was any good."

"Were you, like, Special Forces?" Stan asked.

Charlie laughed.

"It didn't *feel* too special," he said, which didn't really seem like an answer.

Stan decided not to press him on it anymore right then.

"Thanks for teaching us, Charlie," he said instead. "I mean, I know you're getting paid and everything, but still. Thanks. This is really cool. Coolest thing I've ever done, actually."

"Yeah, I agree," Elpidia said, a smile coming to her lips.

Charlie nodded thoughtfully, not saying anything at first. He dropped his head and looked at the sand.

For a second, Stan thought he had said something wrong.

But when Charlie brought his head back up, he was smiling, too.

"It's nice havin' y'all out here," he said. "The visitors I usually get aren't as good company, that's for sure."

Stan glanced at Elpidia, confused, but she just shrugged.

Neither of them were sure what that meant.

9

"Sometimes it's hard to tell what is
medicine and what is poison."
—ELPIDIA'S MOM

Charlie had a whole collection of fighting sticks that were
some of the coolest things Elpidia or Stan had ever seen.
A lot of them, Charlie said, he'd brought back with him
from the Philippines. They were made of a special kind
of wood called "rattan," and they came in matching sets
of two, each one about two and a half feet long. Charlie
had some that looked like miniature tree trunks that had
been cut down and sawed off at both ends. He had others
where the wood was smooth and polished and shiny and
dark. Some of the sticks had designs on them. One of the

sets had the shape of dark scorpions, like shadows, burned over the wood.

He showed Elpidia and Stan where he kept most of them, in his garage, but he wouldn't let either of his new students handle them, and definitely not practice with them.

"Why not?" Elpidia had asked.

"Because you'll break each other's hands or heads or, worse, you'll break *my sticks*, and then I'll have broken sticks, and your lola and your mama won't pay me to teach you anymore."

Instead Charlie gave them tubes of thick cardboard around which he'd wrapped what looked and felt like packing foam. It was held to the tubes with strips of heavy tape. They each got one. The tubes were as long and just about as thick as the real sticks he'd shown them.

"I'll let you whack a fence post with a real stick at the end of today if you do good with your drills," Charlie promised them both.

The drills he started them off with were simple enough to learn. He showed them how to swing their stick at the other's stick up high so they touched, and then back the other way low so they touched again. Then he had one of them swing overhead, bringing their stick down like they were going to split the other's head, and he had the one being swung on step to the side, out of the path of the stick, as they pushed away their partner's hand holding that stick.

The important parts, he said, were learning how to hold and swing the stick properly. He showed them how to grip it in their fists near the bottom, or what Charlie called the "punyo" of the stick, but not hold *right* at the bottom. You had to leave a few inches of space between the bottom of your fist and the end of the stick. He showed them how to plant their feet and twist their hips into the swing to give them more power and control. He showed them how to hold the end of the stick before they swung it, what he called "chambering" it, either over your shoulder or under your other arm.

Charlie said the other important part was learning to be aware of danger headed their way, and either blocking it or not being there when it struck.

Stan was starting to understand the triangles and diamonds Charlie dug out of the sand and what Stan thought was the "dance" he'd seen Elpidia doing when his mom first brought him here. The way she'd been moving was also how Charlie showed them to move when they were striking with their practice sticks or dodging the other's stick.

They did the drill for most of an hour, taking turns swinging and blocking. By the end Stan was sweating through his shirt, and his arm was burning from his shoulder to his wrist, and he was so out of breath, he felt like his lungs were going to pop like balloons, but he was having fun. He couldn't believe he was learning how to fight with a stick, and he couldn't believe he was learning it with Elpidia.

Suddenly, Elpidia stopped moving, letting her practice stick drop to one side.

Stan almost smacked her right in the face with his own practice weapon before he managed to stop himself.

"What's wrong?" he asked, breathing hard from all the exercise.

Elpidia was staring past him.

"Do you hear that?"

Stan stopped, trying to breathe more quietly and listening.

It was a loud buzzing. At first Stan thought it sounded like bees, but then he realized it was an engine, roaring and rumbling and not muffled by being inside a car, like it was a motorcycle engine.

They both looked to the open gate of Charlie's compound and saw a helmeted figure on a red-and-orange dirt bike speeding through the gap in the fence. There was a cloud of dust ten feet high behind it as it tore up the sand before skidding to a halt just outside Charlie's house.

The rider took off his helmet with hands covered by

black leather gloves and hung it from one of the handlebars of the dirt bike. He was younger than Stan thought he'd be. He looked like he might even be a senior. He was Mexican, his head was shaved bald, and he had what was trying to be a thin mustache that trailed down and wrapped around his chin in an equally wannabe beard. He was wearing a black tank top and black cargo shorts, with tennis shoes and white socks pulled all the way up to his knees. The gold chain around his neck and the gold watch around his left wrist were shining in the light of the afternoon sun.

The rider had a big tattoo inked into his left cheek. It was a black spider crawling on what looked like a flower, a red rose.

"I know him," Elpidia whispered to Stan.

She sounded almost afraid.

"Who is he?" Stan asked.

"Mezco. He's the leader of Los Cocos."

Stan knew *that* name. It was a gang. There were several kids at their school he knew belonged to it. They liked to mark up the buildings with the name and symbol of the gang, either by painting it on walls or carving it into desks and the lunch tables. Sheriff's deputies were always coming to the school to pull them out and talk to them about some kind of bad thing that had happened.

"He hangs out at Abuela's bar with them sometimes.

She lets them because they never start trouble. Not inside the bar, anyway."

"What's he doing here?" Stan asked.

Elpidia didn't have an answer for that.

Mezco didn't bother to stand up from the seat of his bike. He just sat there, waiting for Charlie to walk his bowlegged walk across the sand to greet him, which he did a moment later.

Charlie slapped a hand into Mezco's. They gripped each other's hand for a second before letting go and bumping their closed fists.

"What you got for me, cocinero?" Mezco asked him.

"You're early," Charlie said. "I'll go get it."

Stan and Elpidia watched as Charlie ambled across the sand toward the tiny shack with its metal chimney pipe. He disappeared through the skinny little door, shutting it closed behind him.

"You two playing army with those sticks or what?" Mezco asked them, leaning forward against the bike's handlebars.

Stan didn't know what to say to that. He wasn't sure he could've talked if he did.

Fortunately, Elpidia didn't have that problem.

"We're practicing," she told him. "Charlie's teaching us escrima."

Mezco nodded thoughtfully.

"Simón. You picked a good teacher. Ol' Charlie's got a lot of scrap for bein' so flaco."

He flicked his chin in Stan's direction.

"Oye, how old are you?"

Again, Stan found it hard to make the words come up through his throat.

After a second, Elpidia elbowed him in the ribs, and it seemed to knock those words loose.

"Twelve. I'm twelve."

Mezco whistled air through his pinched lips, making a sound like he was impressed.

"Big for your age. You must rule the yard at your school."

Elpidia giggled at that.

Stan felt his cheeks burn, and not from all the exercise they'd been doing.

Charlie reappeared from inside the little shack, only now he was holding a package under one arm. Whatever was in it, the package was the size and shape of one of Stan's and Elpidia's old school textbooks, and wrapped in newspaper that had been tied together with rough-looking twine.

He brought the bundle over to Mezco, who stashed it in a bag that was hanging off the side of his bike.

"Same time next week, yeah?" he asked Charlie, who only nodded.

Mezco grabbed his helmet and began fitting it back over his bald head.

"Oye, Big Boy!" he called to Stan. "When Charlie decides you're ready to graduate, come see me. I'm always looking for new talent, and we could use a white face to front for us when the sheriff comes around to give us static."

Stan blinked in surprise, not even sure at first that Mezco was talking to him, and he definitely didn't understand how he could help someone like Mezco with the sheriff.

"You can bring your girlfriend," Mezco added.

Elpidia frowned at that, crossing her arms angrily.

Stan almost wanted to say sorry to her, even though he wasn't the one who said it.

They all watched the leader of Los Cocos fire up the dirt bike's engine and spin the thing around, speeding back through the gate the way he'd come.

"What was that, Charlie?" Elpidia asked as the dust settled in Mezco's wake. "What did you give him?"

"A birthday present," Charlie answered. "Now get back to your drills. Both of you. You want to swing a real stick today, right?"

He walked back into the house before Elpidia could question him further.

Stan didn't know what to say. She still looked mad.

It wasn't at him, though.

"I'm sorry I laughed," Elpidia said. "When he said the thing about running the yard."

Stan shrugged. "It's okay. I'm used to it."

Elpidia reached out and touched his arm, just with the tips of a few fingers, but it made Stan stand up straighter and stare at her more intensely.

"No, seriously," she insisted, louder and more forcefully this time. "I mean it. I'm sorry. I wasn't trying to laugh at you. Nobody should laugh at you."

"Thanks," Stan said, and he meant it.

"You *could* run the yard if you wanted to. He's right. You're big enough. You're just not like that. You're not a tool like my cousin who needs to beat on people to feel important."

"I feel like you'd be better at running the yard," Stan told her. "You're a lot tougher than me."

"Yeah, but I'm not big. Maybe we should run it together. You be big, and I'll be tough."

Stan nodded. "Sounds like a plan to me."

They laughed at that, both of them. It was the first real laugh they'd shared together.

Stan would remember that more than any of the escrima lessons they learned that day.

10

"When you're cooking,
you have to control how hot the fire is.
That's the most important thing.
You can't let the fire get away from you."
—ABUELA

Stan didn't know exactly how many houses there were in Lakeshore Estates, but he knew there weren't nearly as many as there should be. He'd been aware since he was even younger than he was now that neighborhoods in Lakeshore didn't look anything like the ones you saw on television. Some streets only had one house on the entire block. Other streets had three or four houses built right next door to each other with nothing else around them, which looked even weirder to Stan. The rest was desert, which he thought probably looked the same as it had before any people had come here. There were no green grass lawns or backyards. The yards in front of Lakeshore houses were nothing but sand and rocks.

Even the actual streets themselves didn't look like any others Stan had ever seen. They had gray concrete pavement on them like a normal street, but you could barely see it for all the sand and tiny little pebbles that covered them. If you fell riding a bike down one of those, you'd tear yourself to shreds.

Stan remembered his mom telling him most of the houses in Lakeshore had been built in the 1960s and 1970s. Stan felt like he remembered seeing one or two new ones being built when he was *really* little, but that seemed like a long time ago.

No one moved to the desert. You were born there because your parents lived there. Stan didn't know many people who'd ever moved *out* of the desert, either.

He was walking alongside Elpidia up the middle of Coachella Drive. One of the good things about so few houses was it also meant you barely ever saw a car driving around the streets. It was safe to walk or play right in the middle of any one you chose.

Elpidia's grandmother had offered to drive him to and from practice with Charlie since Stan and Elpidia trained at the same time. After bringing them back, Abuela instructed them to "go play," which Elpidia obviously took offense to, but she knew better than to argue with Abuela.

"Going and playing" in the desert usually just meant walking around the desert. There wasn't much else to do for kids that was legal.

Stan was telling Elpidia about the book he'd been reading, explaining the story and the characters.

In the middle of it, without really thinking, he mentioned one of his favorite chapters was like a story he was working on.

"You write stories?" Elpidia asked, interrupting him.

"Uh. Yeah. A little."

"Can I read some?"

Stan felt his heart beat faster. He never let anyone read his stories, barely even his mom, and then only when she bugged him relentlessly about it.

"I mean . . . I guess? Maybe, when I finish something good enough."

"Not trying to embarrass you," Elpidia said, rolling her eyes at him with a grin. "I just think it's cool you write stories."

"Thanks," he managed to say, mostly because he didn't know what else to say.

They walked for a while without talking about anything else.

Stan was trying to think of a story he'd written that he wouldn't be embarrassed to have her read. He had notebooks full of them, but the thought of Elpidia being the one to read them made Stan feel like none of those stories were good enough.

He was going to ask her what kind of stories she *liked*, but when Stan turned to her, Elpidia had this weird look on her face, almost like she was in pain.

Before Stan could open his mouth, she began moving faster, walking up ahead of him until she stopped at the edge of the street in front of a foul-smelling lot Stan had never seen before.

"Oh my god," he said when he'd caught up to her. "What happened here?"

They were looking at what used to be a house. What was left was nothing but burnt-black pieces of wood and what looked like sections of a roof that had crumbled down into the rest of the place.

"This was where I used to live," she told him. "It burned down before school started again."

"I remember seeing the smoke!" Stan said, the memory hitting him. "From my house. We couldn't see where it was coming from, but it was black. I asked my mom what she thought it was. She said she hoped someone was burning a bunch of trash or something."

Elpidia laughed a little, but it was a lot like when Stan's father laughed. There was no joy in the sound, no feeling of happiness. It wasn't a real laugh.

"That's kind of true, I guess, yeah."

"What happened?" Stan asked.

Elpidia shrugged. "I still don't really know. It was probably an accident. I don't think either of them did it on purpose."

"Who didn't?"

"My mom and dad."

"Oh."

"Abuela said the firefighters told her it was probably a pipe they were smoking or something. There was a lot of paper and trash around. No one really cleaned up unless I did it."

Stan didn't know what to say to that. He'd never really thought about Elpidia's family besides her grandmother.

She kept talking, but she wasn't looking at Stan. It was almost like she was talking to herself.

"They both always drank a lot, you know? I remember that from way back. We'd have these big parties with the whole family, and there'd be beer cans everywhere, and by the end of it, they'd both be passed out somewhere. The rest of the family, my uncles and everyone, thought it was funny. I remember them laughing about my dad falling asleep on the toilet one time."

That didn't sound all that funny to Stan.

"I don't remember when they started doing the other stuff. I don't remember which one of them started it. I just remember one day there were these bottles of pills all over the table in the living room. That's when I knew things had changed. Pretty soon they were both doing it all the time. My dad lost his job first. They both just kinda . . . stopped. Stopped being them. Stopped even living, pretty much. They never left the couch the last year before the fire."

"Did they . . . in the fire . . ."

"No, the firefighters pulled them out before they burned up. They were lucky."

Elpidia practically spat out the word "lucky."

"You weren't here when it started?"

"No, I was at school. When I came home . . ."

Her eyes weren't seeing what was in front of them anymore. Elpidia was seeing what had happened in the past, probably that day.

"I'm sorry," Stan said.

"It's okay," Elpidia told him, and he could tell that was a lie. "It was a crappy house, anyway. And Mom and Dad had sold pretty much everything we had that was worth anything by then. All I lost was some clothes. Some old dolls. Everything I had that was important I'd hide at Abuela's place."

"What happened to them after the fire? Your mom and dad?"

"Jail. Both of them. Different jails. The cops came, too, not just the fire department. Turns out they weren't getting those pills from a doctor. Big surprise, right?"

There wasn't really any sidewalk on either side of the streets in Lakeshore, but there was a concrete curve that ran along both sides of the streets, gutters for when it rained. Not that it ever seemed to rain.

Elpidia sank down and sat on the edge where the gutter met the sand.

After a moment, Stan sat down next to her.

"That's when everything with my cousins started," Elpidia explained. "My dad is Cahuilla. He was born on the reservation, and he lived there until they got married. My mom is Abuela's daughter. My dad's family always blamed her for taking him away, but everyone pretty much got along until . . ."

Stan nodded. He understood what she meant.

"Anyway, Dad's side of the family all think it's my mom's fault they started doing everything they did. Everybody on my mom's side except Abuela blames my dad for it. No one from either side will talk to anyone from the other. Everyone's *so* mad."

She was finally done talking, it seemed like. Elpidia wasn't crying, but Stan thought that was only because she was holding back the tears.

"I don't really have any family except for my mom," he said. "And my . . . dad. I know I have uncles and aunts and cousins somewhere, but we don't ever . . . we never see them or talk to them. My . . . my dad doesn't let my mom talk to her people. And I get the feeling my dad's people don't want to talk to him."

Stan reached up and gently put his hand on her shoulder.

"Parents can be . . . yeah."

Elpidia looked at his hand on her, then up at his face.

"You're not gonna try to, like, kiss me or something, are you?" she asked, kind of laughing as she said it.

"What? No!" Stan said, his cheeks flushing red with embarrassment. "No! I just . . . I'm sorry about how things are, that's all."

"I'm just messing with you," she told him.

"Oh."

Elpidia leaned her head against his shoulder, scooting closer to him on the sand.

Stan watched her, not moving himself. He didn't know what to do, but decided he didn't really need to do anything. The best thing, he figured, was just to be there for her however she needed or wanted him to be. And it seemed like she just needed his shoulder not to move.

Besides, right then her head resting against him felt better than he imagined a kiss ever could.

11

"Dollar Tacos Every Tuesday After
5:00 p.m.! Al Pastor! Lomo Saltado!"
—*CANTINA VOLCÁN TRADITIONAL*

Abuela and Elpidia's grandfather bought the bar when Elpidia's mom and her brothers were still little kids. It had been called Zip's back then, and it was Abuela who renamed it Cantina Volcán because she'd grown up near a big volcano that, thankfully, never erupted. The cantina was located just across the train tracks that bordered Lakeshore Estates, in a long parking lot that was the only collection of businesses for miles.

Elpidia spent most of her days after school and on weekends helping Abuela in the cantina's kitchen, and she liked it that way. She was trying to learn everything she could about cooking and about how to run a kitchen. She wrote it all down in the notebook she kept about the food truck she was going to have one day.

Today Abuela was teaching her how to prepare everything for their papas a la huancaína, one of their best-selling dishes and one of Abuela's favorites. It was boiled potatoes covered in a spicy queso fresco, a cheese sauce. There was a pot of rich, milky cheese melting and bubbling.

The yellow chili peppers she had grilling on the flattop stove stung her nose. The peppers were called ajíes amarillos, and they came from Peru. Abuela sent Tío Raymond all the way to a market in Mecca just to get them. Abuela was born and grew up in Mexico, in a place called Colima, but her family came from Peru, and she'd learned to make a lot of Peruvian dishes from her mother.

The peppers were the part of the recipe you had to pay the closest attention to. They had seeds inside them, and little ridges called "ribs." If you left the seeds and ribs in them, it made the sauce way too hot for a lot of their customers. Abuela didn't like there to be too little heat either, though. So Elpidia had to be very exact in just how much of the seeds she scooped out and how much of the ribs she cut away.

Serving food like they did also meant the place could

be considered a restaurant instead of just a bar, and because of that kids could hang out there and not only adults. That was a good thing because there was really nothing else for kids to do around Lakeshore Estates. There was nowhere for them to go after school that was designed for them. It led to a lot of the local kids getting into trouble for breaking in and vandalizing different places or doing dumb things like setting off fireworks or starting fires in the desert.

Elpidia's grandparents even put in some arcade machines for the kids who came to the cantina.

"While those are grilling and your cheese is melting," Abuela instructed her, watching Elpidia's every movement, "chop up your onions and your garlic, and peel and slice those eggs we hard-boiled before."

It was a lot to do all at once, but Elpidia was getting good at switching back and forth between tasks. The eggs would go on top of the dish when it was finished. The onions and garlic she chopped up with a sharp kitchen knife were for the queso fresco, she knew.

"Chop the onions a little smaller," Abuela instructed her. "They'll blend up more easy that way."

Elpidia nodded, keeping her eyes on her knife work. The last time she'd look away from the blade while she was using it, Abuela had whacked her on the butt with her cane. Not too hard, but it still hurt.

"Okay," her grandmother announced when Elpidia was done. "Now take everything and put it in the blender. Then it'll be queso fresco."

This was one of Elpidia's favorite parts. She dumped the cheese, peppers, and other ingredients she'd prepped into the plastic container part of the kitchen's blender, working the motor and watching everything swirl and whip and get beaten into a single smooth concoction.

"When I was a little girl," Abuela said, "we used a batán to make all of this. That's a stone grinder. No electric. You used your hand. After a few hours, your hand would feel dead from working that thing. You're lucky to be spoiled with all of this fancy equipment, like that blender."

"Yes, Abuela," Elpidia said mechanically, keeping her eyes on the mixture in the blender, making sure the thickness looked just right.

When she'd finished the queso fresco, Abuela let Elpidia experiment with her own dishes, as long as she kept them small and didn't get in anyone else's way. Lately Elpidia had been interested in making ceviches, which was any kind of raw seafood that you soaked in citrus fruit juice like lime. The natural acids in the juice sort of "cooked" the fish so you didn't need to use a stove or any fire. Elpidia found that fascinating. Today she was using a filet of a white fish she'd cut into small pieces, along with red onion, carrot, and avocado.

The cantina didn't even have a proper kitchen when Elpidia's family took it over. Her grandparents built one out back themselves, adding to it and buying more and new equipment as they were able. It was the food that made the place what it was today, more than just a local bar for a few regular customers from the Estates. People drove for miles to the little deserted-looking strip mall just to eat Abuela's dishes, a lot of which you couldn't find most other places around.

The cantina also served the kind of Mexican food a lot of people expected. They had a whole make-your-own taco bar that was popular. Customers could choose from hot metal bins of different meats. They kept fresh, home-made corn tortillas in a steamer. There were almost twenty different toppings and salsas, all of it made in the kitchen from scratch.

Elpidia was just starting to add the lime juice to her fish when Flavio muscled his way through the kitchen door, a huge plastic tub filled with dirty dishes between his arms.

Flavio had been the busboy at the cantina for as long as Elpidia could remember. He was practically part of their family, like another annoying uncle Elpidia could have done without.

"There's a lost-looking white boy out front asking for

our Elpidia," he said as he moved to the kitchen's huge, deep sink and deposited the plastic tub. "You got a boyfriend now, pequita?"

Elpidia rolled her eyes. "*Why* does everyone have to make jokes about that?"

She'd told Stan he should come by the cantina and see what she and Abuela and the other cooks did, since he'd seemed interested in how a professional kitchen is run. And he definitely seemed interested in eating their food.

Elpidia quickly rinsed her hands off and wiped them on the small apron Abuela had given her when she started working in the kitchen.

"Es muy gordo," Flavio added.

"Don't call him that!" Elpidia snapped at the busboy.

Elpidia went to the door separating them from the rest of the cantina and peeked out of the kitchen. She looked around the front of the cantina and spotted Stan lingering near the front doors, looking nervous as he examined the collection of coin-operated machines they kept there that dispensed stuff like little rubber bouncing balls and temporary tattoos.

"Stan!" she called to him, stepping out into the front of the cantina near the bar. "Over here!"

He looked relieved when he saw her waving to him. Stan finally peeled himself away from the front door and walked across the cantina to meet her.

"Órale, Big Boy!" a familiar voice called out to Stan halfway there.

It was Mezco. He was sitting at a table in the cantina with three other members of Los Cocos. One of them, an eighth grader, Elpidia recognized from their school.

Stan stopped, staring at Mezco like someone had shone a big spotlight on Stan while he was trying to sneak through the darkness.

"I thought that was you," Mezco said. "Charlie's top student."

Elpidia frowned, watching the exchange from over the bar. She didn't know *how* Mezco had decided that.

"You want an empanada?" the gang's leader asked Stan, offering him one of the golden brown pastries filled with cooked beef and chopped tomato and green olives.

Elpidia moved around the bar, walking across the cantina floor until she was standing between Stan and the Los Cocos' table.

"He can't," she told Mezco. "He's supposed to help me in the kitchen. My abuela's waiting."

Mezco nodded slowly as he seemed to consider Elpidia.

He was looking at her like he wasn't sure he liked how she was talking to him.

"All right, then," he finally said. "Don't ever wanna

keep Abuela waiting. Especially yours. The chancla is strong with that one."

The other Cocos laughed.

"Stan, c'mon," Elpidia urged him, seeing he was doing his thing where he just stood there, not sure what to do.

After a while he finally nodded, turning away from Mezco and the others and walking to Elpidia, who held the kitchen door open for him.

"I didn't mean to bug you while you're, like, working or whatever."

Elpidia shook her head, following him into the kitchen.

"I *told* you to come, weirdo."

"I know, I just mean . . . never mind."

Elpidia ignored him like she was learning to do when he acted all shy and weird.

"So, this is where we make everything," she said, leading him down the row of countertops and stoves.

"Hola, mijo," Abuela greeted Stan without looking up from the pot she was stirring. "Don't touch anything, and do what Elpidia tells you. I don't want you to burn yourself."

"Yes, ma'am," Stan said automatically. "Thank you."

Abuela nodded, like she approved of how he spoke to her.

"Nice boy. Get him something to eat, mija."

Flavio burst through the kitchen door again, only this

time he wasn't holding his plastic tub.

Elpidia thought he looked upset.

"Señora," Flavio said to her grandmother. "The sheriff is here again."

"You two stay here," Abuela ordered the kids, grabbing her cane from its resting place. "And watch my soup."

Elpidia and Stan waited until Abuela had left the kitchen, and then they both ran to the kitchen door at the same time.

They didn't open it all the way, just enough for both of them to see into the front of the cantina.

Sheriff McCann was a big man, almost as tall as Charlie and twice his size through the chest and shoulders. He was going bald, and he tried to comb his orange/red hair to cover it up. He had two deputies with him, both younger-looking guys, both white with thick mustaches like him.

The three of them were standing over the gang members huddled around their table.

The rest of the cantina had become quiet. Everyone who wasn't watching what was happening was pretending not to watch what was happening.

Elpidia's grandmother leaned on her cane as she walked over to the three, taking her time.

"Is there a problem, Sheriff?" Abuela asked McCann.

"Not yet," he said, barely looking down at the small

elderly woman. "Just having a conversation with my friend Albert here."

"That's not my name," Mezco corrected him coolly.

"Oh, I'm sorry, I get confused," the sheriff apologized, but it was clear he didn't mean it. "Your name's not Albert Marquez. These other boys are part of your church choir, not your gang. And none of you know anything about all those trucks that keep getting broken into at the truck stop up Route Eighty-Six, right? That's me being confused again."

Mezco shrugged, shaking his head.

"We ride bikes, not trucks. Know what I mean?"

Sheriff McCann nodded. "Yeah, I gotcha, Albert."

Abuela cleared her throat loudly to get his attention.

"If you want to talk to them about official police business, I would prefer you did it outside," she told him without the slightest bit of fear or hesitation in her voice. "Because otherwise you are just bothering my customers, and I won't have that."

McCann looked annoyed. His lips got tight, and the skin of his forehead wrinkled.

But he didn't talk back to Abuela. He just nodded slowly without saying a word.

"Have some beers on the house before you go," she offered.

"Flavio!" Abuela shouted at the busboy. "¡Cervezas para la juda!"

Mezco and his boys snickered at that.

Fortunately neither the sheriff nor his deputies spoke Spanish.

"We're all on duty, ma'am, but thank you," McCann said to Abuela politely.

"We'll see you and your boys around, Albert," the sheriff said to Mezco, and it sounded like a threat.

"Simón, Jefe," Mezco said, and if he was scared or bothered, he didn't show it. "Let's do lunch some time."

The other Cocos laughed again.

That made the sheriff and both of his deputies mad. Elpidia could see them stiffen up where they stood, frowning and narrowing their eyes. She was worried for a second they might do something that would lead to a big fight in the cantina, which she knew was the last thing Abuela wanted or that the business needed.

Instead, the sheriff leaned slowly between Mezco and the gang member sitting next to him. McCann reached down and picked up one of their empanadas.

Staring at Mezco, he began stuffing the whole thing in his mouth all at once until it disappeared. McCann sucked at the fingertip that pushed the last bit in and then chewed the empanada up and swallowed it.

"That's delicious," he said to Abuela.

The sheriff turned around and began walking toward the cantina doors. He waved at his deputies to follow him.

Nobody said or did anything until all three of them were gone and the doors were closed behind them.

It was like waiting for a bad smell to clear out of a room.

"Gracias, señora," Mezco said to Abuela.

Elpidia's grandmother looked at the gang leader and frowned.

She tapped the bottom of her cane against the cantina floor a few times.

"You boys disappoint me," she said, turning and letting her cane guide her steps back to the kitchen.

Elpidia and Stan both moved away from the door, looking at each other with worry and confusion in their eyes.

Neither of them said anything as Abuela limped past them, returning to her soup pot.

"That was crazy," Stan finally whispered to Elpidia.

Elpidia just shook her head.

"It's like I always say. This town is just too small."

12

"Knowing what someone has done
doesn't mean you know who they are.
It took me a long time to learn
those are two different things."
—*SHERIFF MCCANN*

"Faster!" Elpidia shouted, and laughed at Stan over the *tap-tap-tap* of their sticks. "C'mon! Fast as you can!"

Stan double-timed the speed with which he was moving his arms and swinging his sticks. He was starting to breathe like a thirsty dog, and the upper parts of his arms were aching, but he made sure he matched each strike Elpidia made against her target.

The sun was scorching, and Stan was grateful for the bandannas he'd started making out of his old shirts that didn't fit anymore. He wore them tied snugly around his forehead to soak up his sweat. There was a lot of it. He usually hated how much he sweated, but during training he didn't mind so much. It even felt good. The same was true for the heat. He'd always hated how hot it was in the Estates, but training in that heat made it burn in a different way that made him feel alive.

He and Elpidia practiced the Heaven and Earth drill on two spindly, crooked little trees barely taller than they were. Each of them held sticks in both hands, chambering one while swinging the other at their tree's peeling bark, then switching sticks and doing it over again. Charlie said it was called Heaven and Earth because of the way they held their sticks with the ends pointed up toward the sky.

With each movement, Stan and Elpidia tapped the trees with the end of their sticks at the same time, almost like they were performing a choreographed dance.

When they'd first started doing the drill, they'd each leave marks all over the bark of the trees, as if a wild dog had been gnawing on the trunks. Now, every strike landed in almost the same spot. Instead of little nicks in the bark, they were taking huge chunks out of the sides of both trees.

Even Stan, who never used to think he was good at much of anything, couldn't deny he was getting *good* at this. His arms felt stronger than they ever had before. His hands were fast, and his aim was good. And his muscles were starting to remember the movements on their own. It felt like he barely had to think or concentrate on what he was doing.

Stan's arms finally gave out on him, and he had to stop performing the drill. He bent forward at the waist, digging the ends of his sticks into the sand and leaning on them while he tried to catch his breath.

He could hear Elpidia giggling, but it didn't hurt his feelings because he knew she wasn't laughing *at* him.

"You're getting a lot better at keeping up!" she said between bursts of laughter.

"Thanks," Stan managed, coughing around the word as he tried to catch his breath.

"Sticks down, stick fighters!" Charlie called to them from the middle of his patchwork compound. "I got medicine for you!"

Stan and Elpidia ran over to where he was standing with two plastic bottles of Gatorade for them.

"I been keeping it cold in the ice cooler for y'all," he said. "You've been workin' hard."

Elpidia and Stan both thanked him, gratefully taking the bottles and greedily cracking open the tops before gulping down the Gatorade at the same time.

Charlie watched them with a strange smile on his face, Stan thought, almost like he was dreaming of something, even though Charlie was clearly awake.

Elpidia found a car engine block left to rust in the sand to sit on.

Stan followed her lead and plunked down on a big old television with nothing inside of it.

"Why do you keep all this junk around?" Stan asked their teacher.

"This ain't junk!" Charlie protested, pretending like he was deeply offended by Stan's comment. "This is raw material. I built this whole place out of things like that. And it was all free, gifts of the desert. You never know when spare parts will come in handy."

Stan hadn't thought about it like that. He didn't know how to build things. His mom said that Stan's dad did construction when Stan was little, but he'd never taught Stan how to do any of it.

"Charlie, are we the first kids you've taught?" Elpidia asked.

"The first *kids*, yeah," he said. "Why?"

"Nothing. I was just thinking, you said you came out here to get away from everybody."

"That's true."

"So then . . . why did you agree to teach us?"

Charlie shrugged off the question. "You gotta use what you know to make your way in this world. I only know a few things folks think is worth their dollars."

Stan didn't believe that, though, at least the part about money being the reason he agreed to teach them. Maybe it was one of the reasons, but Stan knew Charlie had only been paid a small part of what he was owed for all of Stan's lessons so far. Charlie was letting Stan's mom owe him that money, and he didn't seem to care much when or if she ever gave it to him.

"If you never taught kids before," Elpidia said, sounding like she was just beginning to put pieces of a puzzle together, "how did Abuela know you'd teach me?"

"Your lola . . . she helped me, a long time ago, before you even," Charlie explained. "When I first came out here, before I built this place. All I had was what I could fit in the back of that old truck over there. I spent my last dollar in your family's cantina. Your lola kind of took me in. She gave me trust and kindness. I still don't know why, really. But I'll always be grateful."

Elpidia looked surprised. "She never said anything."

Charlie shrugged again. "After I built up all this, I kinda stopped coming into town."

Stan couldn't stop thinking about Charlie's answer to the question of why he was teaching them, about the money.

"You didn't owe my mom anything, though," he pointed out.

"No, but she's a good lady, and just like Elpidia's lola, she was kind to me."

Charlie stopped all of a sudden, like he was going to say more, but decided not to at the last second.

Stan looked at Elpidia, and it was clear she'd noticed it too.

Neither of them said anything more. They looked at Charlie, waiting.

He stayed silent for a minute longer, but eventually he said the thing that was on his mind.

"Besides . . . I was feeling being a teacher again, after Elpidia's lola brought her here. And teaching y'all, especially. I suppose I like the idea you'll do something good with it. I never taught anybody who . . . I guess who really *needed* it before. Not the way y'all do. Or the way you *did*, since you're both little warriors now."

Stan and Elpidia laughed at that, but even if they knew it was mostly a joke, the compliment felt real and good.

Charlie laughed with them, but eventually the laughter and his smile faded. The look that replaced them was more serious.

"And maybe I been out here by myself too long," he admitted. "Maybe. Anyway! The day ain't over yet."

They knew what he meant. Stan and Elpidia finished their Gatorades.

Charlie proceeded to carefully wrap their hands in

what he called hemp, which felt like strips of cotton, only tougher and thicker. Once their knuckles and palms and wrists were protected, they practiced their empty hand techniques, which was basically fighting without sticks or any other kind of tools.

Charlie always called them "tools" and not "weapons" because he said even when fighting empty-handed, they both had plenty of weapons. He didn't just mean their fists, either. They'd learned to use their elbows, forearms, the edges of their hands, and even their fingers to strike an opponent.

They started off by attacking the air in front of them, just practicing their form and their stance. Like the stick drills, their bodies remembered exactly how to do everything now without them having to think about it.

Charlie did the empty hand drills with them, correcting and giving them little tips on how to do things better every now and then.

When he was satisfied, he had Stan and Elpidia square off for sparring so they could practice against an opponent. They moved slow so they didn't actually hurt each other, but it helped to have an opponent to block and dodge and make it all feel real. It was also hard to practice joint locks and body holds and throws without an actual person, and that was all the kind of stuff Charlie always said was the best way to end a fight quickly and without getting hurt.

After a while, Charlie left them to train on their own and disappeared into his ramshackle house.

Stan and Elpidia continued to spar for another few minutes, until Elpidia ducked under one of Stan's jabs and jumped up on his back, putting him in a headlock.

Stan ran around like a wild chicken trying to shake her off, both of them laughing the whole time.

She only let go when they saw Charlie walk back out of his front door, both hands behind his back.

"I got something for y'all," he told them, kneeling in the sand between Stan and Elpidia.

"You won't get no blue or black or red belt from me like if you went to some martial arts class in a mall. I've told y'all before, you're either trained or you're untrained. That's it. You don't need no other rank or badge or ribbon or whatever. You both got a *lot* to learn still, but I'd say we can call you trained. So, this is what I made to mark the occasion."

He held a fist out to each of them and opened his hands. Resting atop each of Charlie's palms was a small oval-shaped pendant, like something that would hang from a necklace. They were flat on the bottom, but had a round dome of what looked like clear glass on top.

Under the glass of each was a tiny, perfectly preserved, very real scorpion. It was like Charlie's belt, except he'd arranged the scorpion in Elpidia's pendant so its claws and tail kind of made an "E," for her name, and he'd twisted Stan's scorpion into what looked exactly like an "S."

It was weird and cool at the same time.

"That is so wicked, thank you," Stan said, taking his scorpion pendant and running his hand over the smooth surface of the glass.

"Thanks, Charlie," Elpidia echoed, holding hers cupped in both hands.

"And who knows, maybe they help y'all remember me when you get big and go out into the world."

Stan looked at Elpidia, not wanting to speak for her, but also thinking she'd feel the same way he did about this.

"We could never forget you, Charlie," he said.

Elpidia didn't say anything, but she nodded like she really meant it.

Charlie smiled that dreamy smile again. He put his right hand over his heart and bowed to them both.

Stan and Elpidia returned the salute, holding the pendants he'd made them over their hearts as they did.

Stan hadn't really meant to do that, but it felt right.

"I'm sorry we don't have anything to give you back," Elpidia said as Charlie slowly stood up from his kneeling position.

"You already gave it to me, iha," he assured her. "You both already did."

13

"You'll never be able to see every
strike coming. You just have to hope
you can recover from it."
—CHARLIE

"I really don't want to do this," Stan said to her for what was probably the fourth time that morning.

"You told me you came to train with Charlie because you're scared all the time, right? And this is one of the things you're scared of, right? Well, what's the point of training if you're going to stay scared of stuff."

Stan was regretting having admitted all of that to her. He'd only told his mom to get her to agree to find him someone to teach him to fight. He didn't know why he'd said any of that to Elpidia when they were practicing drills at Charlie's place.

For some reason it was easy to tell her things, even private things. Once Stan got over the nervousness of first being around Elpidia, he found he liked talking to her, and that he felt comfortable sharing what he thought and how he felt about pretty much anything and everything.

They were waiting for the school bus in a vacant concrete lot with about fifteen other kids of all different ages and grades. None of them really knew why the giant square of pavement was there, surrounded by nothing but empty desert. Maybe someone was going to build something and they decided to start with the parking lot first, but then they either ran out of money or decided building *anything* out here was a waste of time.

In either case, the lot had been there as long as Stan or Elpidia could remember, and that was where kids who lived in Lakeshore Estates waited for the bus. There was no sign that said so, but it had always been that way. A lot of things people did in the desert seemed to be because they were just used to doing them.

Stan couldn't remember the last time he'd been on the lot, but his hatred of the bus hadn't changed. Waiting there was making him sweat, and all he was doing was sitting still.

"It's gonna be *fine*," Elpidia assured him, seeing how he was sweating and freaking out. "We'll find a seat together. Just relax."

He thought of something new and scary in a totally different way.

"Your cousins don't take this bus, do they?" he asked.

"No. They get driven in from the reservation. Don't worry."

He *was* worried, though. The last time he'd tried to take the bus, the time that made him finally give it up and start walking, he hadn't even been able to find a seat. He'd walked up and down the aisle twice, and no one would make room for him. A couple of them called him out in front of everyone for being fat. A few others made fun of him for being fat and white and slow. The next thing Stan knew, the whole bus was laughing at him. He ended up running away, trying not to cry but not able to stop himself. He didn't even go to school that day.

No one had messed with him at the stop so far, and he was surprised. It must've been that Elpidia was hanging out with him. Nothing else had changed about him except that.

The bus finally arrived. The driver, a burly guy in a blue work shirt and a darker blue sweater vest, didn't even see them as they all piled inside, hiking up the steps into the bus. It was early in the morning, but it was already hot outside, and the bus didn't have any air-conditioning (although the driver had a little fan up front just for him,

Stan always noticed). It smelled like corn chips and someone's dirty socks.

When he'd ridden the bus in the past, he always hoped there was still an empty seat by the time it got to their vacant lot in the Estates. If not, Stan would try to find a seat that had one little kid in it from a lower grade who wouldn't say anything to him and was small enough that they wouldn't be too crowded.

The bus was full that morning, and Stan felt like everyone was staring at him. No one had said anything yet, but he could see what they were thinking just by the way their eyes looked.

Stan stopped walking halfway down the aisle. The farther into the bus they went, the more his stomach twisted into painful knots. The back of the bus was where all the older kids sat, and they were the worst ones.

Elpidia finally had to grab him by his backpack strap and pull him forward to get him moving again.

"Here," she announced quietly to him, pulling him by the same strap into an empty seat about five rows from the very back.

Stan felt relief, but only for a second. He could hear some of the older kids yelling at him from the back and laughing.

"Just ignore them," Elpidia said. "They'll get bored and think of something else do to if you don't do anything."

"You sound like my mom," Stan grumbled.

"She must be a smart lady."

Stan felt something touch the back of his head. A second later his ear started to feel wet.

"Aw, man . . ." he started to groan.

"It's just a spitball," Elpidia said, examining his hair. "I hope it's just spit, anyway."

"¡Estúpido!" Elpidia hollered back at them venomously. "Knock it off before I come back there and stomp you out!"

Before Stan could say anything, she actually snatched the spitball from out of his hair and hurled it at the back of the bus.

Elpidia stood up on the seat beside him and turned to stare down the length of the bus, almost daring whoever made the spitball to say or do something back to her.

Stan heard some giggles, but otherwise no one took her up on the challenge.

Elpidia sunk back into the seat next to Stan. She looked like she was about to say something to him, but instead she suddenly looked at the hand she'd used to throw back the spitball.

"Ew!" she groaned, only then seeming to realize what she'd just done.

Elpidia wiped her hand against his shirt, her face twisted in fake pain.

Stan couldn't help but laugh.

The laughing didn't last long, though.

"They all really hate me," Stan said, more to himself than to her.

"They don't hate *you*. They just hate what you are."

"What, a fat kid?"

"No. I mean, they're jerks about that, too, but I meant all they see when they look at you is a gringo."

Stan knew the word.

"Yeah. So?"

Elpidia sighed. "Stan . . . did you ever notice that everyone in charge of anything around here—our teachers, the sheriff and his deputies, the people who run the farms and the shops . . . pretty much everyone except Abuela with the cantina—they're *all* white."

Hearing her say that hit Stan harder than the spitball had. Because it wasn't something he'd ever thought about or would have noticed, even.

He didn't know what that had to do with the other kids hating him, either.

Elpidia must have recognized the confused look on his face.

"You remember what Mezco said to you the first time we met him?" she reminded Stan. "About having a 'white face' in his gang?"

Stan nodded. That certainly wasn't a conversation he'd ever forget.

"And you remember how the sheriff talked to them in the cantina?" Elpidia asked. "How he treated them like they were already guilty? The way my grandmother had to step in? What do you think could've happened to them if she hadn't been there, or if they hadn't all been in the cantina?"

Stan thought about that. It had been clear how much Sheriff McCann hated Mezco and his boys. Stan remembered thinking the sheriff looked like he wanted to hurt them. Not just arrest them or put them in jail, but physically hurt them all.

"But what could I do to help—" Stan began to say, only for Elpidia to cut him off.

"Most of the people who live and work out here look like me," she said. "But the people who tell them what to do all look like you. There's way more of us than them, but they get to be in charge. And they only listen to other white people. You think that's just because white people are smarter or better or something?"

"No."

"Right."

"Well, I'm not in charge of anything. I can't tell anyone what to do."

"I didn't say it was fair. That's the point, I guess. None of how things are around here is fair. I'm just telling you that's why. A lot of the other kids are just jerks. But the rest . . . I dunno, if you watched all your family get treated like they watch their parents and aunts and uncles get treated and couldn't do anything about it, it'd probably make you feel good to give it back to someone who looked like the people who messed with your family every day. Even if it's just a kid who can't do anything about it, like you."

"I never thought of it like that before. I'm sorry."

"I'm sorry you're the one poor little gringo in Lakeshore," Elpidia said, sounding like she was half joking.

She nudged him in the side with her elbow.

"I like you, anyway," she told him.

"Thanks."

A second later, Stan said, "I like you, too."

Elpidia grinned up at him.

"Why wouldn't you? I'm awesome."

The rest of the ride wasn't bad. In fact, after a while Stan forgot how much he hated the bus. He forgot to be nervous and afraid and uncomfortable.

He just hung out with his friend and let everyone else fade into the background until he couldn't see or hear them.

14

"You don't just throw a bunch
of ingredients in a pot and hope for
the best. You pick the flavors that make
each other better and stronger than
they are on their own."
—ABUELA

A while ago Elpidia had started sharing her lunch with
Stan every day at school. She was hanging out with
him during most breaks anyway, and when she saw the
junk he had to eat, on the days he even *had* anything to
eat, Elpidia just couldn't take it after a while. Coming
from a family of cooks like she did, she couldn't believe
his mom sent him to school with nothing but sugar-filled
snacks and no other *real* food.

He swore dinners at his house were better. Stan said his
mom just didn't have a ton of money for groceries, and she

did the best she could. He said she also didn't know much about food and cooking besides.

When Elpidia finally told Abuela about the whole situation, the old woman started sending her to class with *two* lunches, one for her and one for Stan. Abuela never actually said the second meal was for Stan. She just started packing extra food one morning and gave it to Elpidia without a word, trusting her to figure it out. That was her grandmother. It was like she only had so many words she was going to be able to speak in her life and she was afraid of using them all up.

That day Elpidia had two plastic containers filled with machaca and eggs left over from the daily meal Abuela made for the staff at the cantina. She and Stan were sitting under one of the gray dead trees that Stan said reminded him of bones on a skeleton. They ate their spicy dried beef and scrambled eggs with plastic forks and talked about an idea they'd had during their last practice at Charlie's place.

"It'd be like a bookstore that's also a restaurant," Stan had said to her. "You could make the food, and I could sell my books. Other books, too. By famous writers, to get people to come."

"People would come for the food," Elpidia assured him. "That's why they come to the cantina. But it'd need to be stuff people can eat while they read, like little snacks and things. Nothing messy, so they don't mark up the books."

Stan was impressed. "Yeah, that's smart!"

"I'm thirsty," Elpidia said. "You thirsty?"

Stan nodded. "Pretty much always."

"I found a quarter in the parking lot outside the cantina this morning. I think with that I have enough for a soda from the machine. You wanna split it?"

"Sure, it'll keep me awake through math later."

That made Elpidia laugh.

She stood up under the tree, not happy about leaving what little shade they had. It was another hot day.

She walked across the old churchyard toward where the school's one soda machine stood against a wall, surrounded by a rusted cage to protect it from being broken into. The machine itself was so old that the soda advertised on the front of it didn't even exist anymore.

Elpidia liked the idea about the bookstore that was also a restaurant. She wasn't sure she liked it as much as her food truck because the whole point was not to get stuck in one place. She'd felt stuck her whole life. But if they picked somewhere cool to open it, that might not be so bad. She liked hearing Stan talk about writing books.

She was so lost in thought, she didn't even hear them coming. The next thing she knew, two big hands were shoving her from behind, and Elpidia was pushed off her feet and down to the ground on all fours. She felt the sharp little rocks covering the old churchyard bite into her hands and knees, cutting her skin.

"Crunchy Girl!" her cousin Marigold yelled like she was happy to see Elpidia.

Elpidia looked over her shoulder. Marigold had the two trolls she called her sisters with her, like always.

Fine, she thought. *Now is when it's going to happen. It had to happen sooner or later—that's why you've been training with Charlie for the last two months. It might as well be now. You're not going to get any more ready.*

Elpidia stood up, wiping blood and sand and pebbles from her knees.

"Marigold," she began, "I really don't hate you. It's not even that I don't like you. But I'm tired of this."

"Oh yeah? What are you gonna do about it?"

Elpidia wished she had a stick, but she was also glad she didn't. She just wanted to show them they couldn't mess with her like they used to, so they'd stop coming at her. She didn't want to put any of her cousins in the hospital.

She got ready, planting her feet the way Charlie had taught her and raising her hands to block and counter-strike when Marigold threw the first punch.

She waited for it.

Before either Marigold or Elpidia could make a move, Stan stepped between them.

Elpidia had forgotten all about him.

Stan was just as tall as Marigold was, despite being two years younger than her.

Suddenly her cousin didn't look so big or scary.

"Stan, stay out of this," Elpidia warned him.

She didn't want him to get hurt, and as big as he was, Elpidia 100 percent believed Marigold and her minions would take Stan down like one of those deer-looking things that lions liked to eat on Nat Geo.

As much as she was worried about him, Elpidia also felt like she had to do this herself. She'd been training for weeks for this moment.

Stan didn't go anywhere, though. He just looked back at her and shook his head.

He had a weird look on his face. Elpidia had never seen him look like that before. Maybe it was because for the first time ever he didn't look nervous or scared.

It was more than that, though. Stan looked the exact opposite of nervous and scared.

That was also when Elpidia became aware they had an audience. It had started with two or three kids stopping what they were doing and turning their heads to watch the scene unfolding between the five of them. Now there was an actual crowd gathered around them in a wide circle. Elpidia could feel dozens of eyes staring at her.

"Listen to your girl, fat boy," Marigold said to Stan. "I've knocked out guys taller than you before."

He looked back at Elpidia's cousin, his voice not shaking even a little as he answered her. Stan ignored the voices getting louder all around them.

"Well, I'm not gonna hit a girl," he said. "So I guess you better go for it if you really want to. Lunch is about to be over soon."

Somehow, and she couldn't even really explain it, Elpidia *knew* Stan saw the punch coming. It was like the whole world went into slow-motion, like in a movie. Elpidia could see everything as it was happening. Stan was watching Marigold's fist fly at his face, and he wasn't doing anything to stop it. He didn't even try to dodge the shot. He didn't move at all, in fact.

Marigold punched Stan with full force, her fist landing against his cheek and part of his eye. Her thick knuckles opened a small cut right next to the end of his eyebrow.

Still, she might as well have punched a wall.

Stan never even flinched. His head didn't turn even a little. He took Marigold's best shot like it was nothing.

He even smiled back at her.

Elpidia's other cousins and the kids who'd gathered

around to watch, who had been yelling and cheering a second ago when they thought a fight was starting, all fell silent.

Marigold didn't know what to do, either. She looked confused and more than a little embarrassed. Stan might as well have just asked her to solve a really complicated math problem. It was like watching all the air go out of an overfilled balloon.

Stan absorbing that punch without reacting to it had changed the mood of everyone, Marigold most of all.

Just like that, the fight was over without ever really starting. Everyone, all the other kids, started drifting away from the scene.

Elpidia felt like there was a chance to do something here, to maybe even end the war between them once and for all.

"Let's just squash this, Marigold," she offered. "Right now. I never had a problem with any of you. I still don't. I didn't want any of what happened to happen. You don't want to be my cousin, that's fine, but let's stop doing this. It's not going to change anything. It's not . . . it's not going to bring him home."

She wasn't sure if Marigold started nodding because she agreed or because she didn't know what else to do.

It was something, at least.

Her cousins started walking away. Elpidia watched and waited. Marigold looked back once, but she didn't turn around.

"You didn't do anything Charlie taught us!" Elpidia whispered hotly to Stan. "You didn't block and counter! You didn't dodge it! You didn't . . ."

"I didn't want to hit her!" he hissed back at her. "And if I'd moved, she just would've kept trying to hit me! I did the only thing I could think of!"

"Well . . . it worked," Elpidia admitted.

"Yeah, I guess it did."

They were both too surprised to say anything else for a minute.

"That is the scariest girl I've ever met," Stan admitted to her, quietly, wiping at the blood on his face without seeming like it even bothered him.

Elpidia had to put a hand over her mouth to keep herself from laughing out loud.

"Are you really okay?" she asked, the words a little muffled as she was talking through her fingers.

"Yeah, I'm fine," he assured her.

"Really?"

Stan immediately shook his head. "No. It hurts *so much*."

This time Elpidia did laugh. She couldn't help it. Not

that she didn't feel bad for him, of course.

"I take it all back," she said. "You did great. Charlie would be proud of you."

"Of us," Stan corrected her.

Elpidia couldn't get over it. She'd imagined how this whole thing was going to play out for weeks. She'd imagined beating up all three of her cousins. She'd imagined them stomping her to death. But she'd never pictured this.

It turned out Elpidia didn't need a pair of rattan fighting sticks to defeat her cousins. She didn't even need the Filipino martial arts skills Charlie had been teaching them.

In the end, she just needed a friend who had her back.

15

"That's one of the things I like about
cooking. You start fresh every day. It
doesn't matter what happened yesterday.
The food you make today is totally new.
You always get a second chance."
—ELPIDIA

Stan had a new idea for a story. It was about a cook in
the future, where everyone lived in floating buildings
high in the sky because the ground had all been destroyed
in a war, and chemicals got poured on it that made it so
people couldn't rebuild or survive down below anymore.
The cook had a hover cart that she flew from window to
window selling food to people, and for ingredients she had
to make do with what she caught in the air, like different
kinds of birds.

Stan didn't know exactly what would *happen* in the

story yet to make it exciting; he just had the character and what she did and the idea for the world. It was a start, though.

He wasn't *trying* to impress Elpidia, not really, but he did hope she'd think it was cool. Stan wasn't going to tell her he was basing the character on her. He just kind of hoped she'd notice on her own, *if* he finished the story, of course.

He was sitting on the floor, leaning against the foot of his bed that barely fit him anymore. He was writing out the first part of the story with a pen in one of his spiral notebooks, crossing out every third word or sentence when he decided he didn't like it, but that was all part of writing.

It was hard to distract Stan when he was writing. He got in a zone in his head where he was *inside* whatever imaginary world he was writing about, and he tuned out everything about the real world when that happened. That had been his favorite thing to do before he met Charlie.

Still, as deep in that zone as he could get, sometimes the real world found a way to break through.

Stan heard his father yelling first. His loud voice carried through the whole of their little crumbling house when he was angry.

Stan's mom yelled back at him. She didn't sound scared, not yet anyway. She sounded just as mad as he did. Stan couldn't make out the words from where he was sitting.

He tossed his notebook and pen behind him onto his bed and crawled across the floor of his bedroom. Stan pressed his ear against his closed door. He wasn't supposed to come out when he heard them yelling. That was his mom's rule, and she'd told it to him a million times. It didn't matter if the yelling turned to screaming and the sounds of glass and furniture breaking—he was never supposed to come out when he was in his room and he heard them fighting.

"Where's the money, then?" his father was demanding. "You've been workin' every Saturday for months now. So where is it? You think I can't count?"

Oh no, Stan thought.

It was about him training with Charlie. His father had finally noticed something wasn't right. His mom had been telling him she was taking Stan to the date farm office with her while she worked extra hours, to explain why they were gone and why she needed the car on Saturdays. Since his father barely noticed when they were home anyway, so far it had all been fine. Stan didn't know why his father was making a big deal about it now.

He must have run out of beer, Stan thought. He was always the worst when he was just drunk enough to still think clearly.

"I'm saving it," he heard his mother lie.

"Saving it *where*?" his father asked in a way that made it clear he didn't believe her.

"What difference does it make, Bill? Have you reached for a beer and not found it lately? Do I not keep you fed? The TV works and the couch is still there. What else do you need? What else do you even care about?"

A second later Stan heard a crash and the ringing of what sounded like metal, like something big had been knocked over onto the floor.

He felt cold in his stomach, and his mouth went painfully dry.

His mom would yell at him to go back to his room, but Stan didn't care. He opened the door, walking down the hall into their living room.

She was lying on the floor next to an end table that usually sat beside the couch. It had an ashtray and some other knickknacks on it that were all over the carpet now.

Stan didn't know whether his father had hit her or pushed her down, and it didn't matter. Neither was okay, he told himself. None of this was ever okay. It had never been okay.

"Where's she been takin' you every Saturday?" his father demanded, his thick chest rising and falling with every breath so hard Stan could see it move.

Stan didn't answer him, but not because he was afraid. He was staring up at his father, and Stan's jaw hurt from how hard his teeth were pressing against each other. Stan felt so angry, and so sick of nights like this.

"Did you *hear* me?!" his father yelled at him.

Charlie had told Stan never to strike an opponent in the neck unless he was ready to do serious damage. The neck and throat were places you could kill someone if you hit them there hard enough or in just the right or wrong spot. He'd shown them ways to use the fighting stick to choke someone so they'd pass out unconscious. Charlie said that kind of move was only to be used if you thought your life was in danger.

If you didn't want to risk attacking your opponent's neck, then Charlie taught them to go for other "soft" spots, the chin and the nose and the eyes.

That's what kept running through Stan's mind at that moment.

Chin, nose, eyes. Chin, nose, eyes.

"I'm ready to be a man," he said.

It actually looked like he'd surprised his father. The old man blinked down at him with cloudy, confused eyes.

Then he laughed, just a little.

His father pointed a finger at Stan, wagging it drunkenly.

"I'm going to hit you so hard, *she's* going to feel it," he said, turning the finger toward Stan's mom for a moment then stabbing the air in front of Stan again. "And then you're going to tell me what's been goin' on behind my back around here."

Grab his finger, the part of Stan's brain where Charlie's training lived instructed him. *Grab his finger and twist it as hard as you can and hold it. Then you go for his face with your other hand. You can ridge-hand him in the nose and gouge his eyes and punch him in the chin . . .*

Except Stan didn't do any of that. He didn't even start backing up as his father stepped toward him.

Stan's own voice was a scream inside his head.

What are you waiting for? Do it! Do it now!

He couldn't. His father seemed to loom even taller over him than usual. He looked as big as a building to Stan. Doing anything to him seemed impossible. It made Stan sick just thinking about it now.

His father could see the fear returning to Stan's eyes. It was like the old man had been waiting for it.

"Look at you," he practically spat at Stan. "You're still a fat little coward. You ain't never gonna be any kind of man."

At least move out of his way, Stan's inside voice begged him. *At least do that. Please.*

132

It was useless, though. Wherever that voice came from, it couldn't move Stan's body for him. He was frozen. None of what Charlie had taught him mattered in that moment. None of the knowledge about fighting and defending himself Stan possessed now and all the practicing he'd done to be able to use it could help him. All he could do was stand there with his arms limp at his sides like he always did when his father got in his face.

Stan knew what was coming, and he wasn't afraid of the pain or being injured. He just hated that he couldn't stop it. He hated that he couldn't even make himself try, even after everything he'd done to get ready for this moment.

His father kicked him in the chest, slamming the bottom of his work boot into Stan like he was a door his father was trying to kick in. All the air went out of Stan, and he felt himself falling, except he wasn't dropping to the floor—he was flying across the room. He smashed into the living room wall so hard, he felt the wall crack and break around his shoulders. The back of his head bounced off the plaster, and his tailbone landed on the carpet so hard, it made his whole back and butt hurt.

He sat there against the wall, dizzy and unable to breathe or move. Everything hurt. His eyes were shut tight, mostly because the light from the living room lamp hurt to look at just then.

"I want to see the money you've been makin'," Stan heard his father yelling at his mom, "or you better tell me some kinda story about what's goin' on that I believe."

The next sound he heard was his father stomping out of the house. A few minutes later, there was the sound of a truck engine firing to life outside, and Stan listened to tires peeling across the sand as his father drove away into the night.

"Stan, open your eyes, honey."

Mom was there. She'd crawled over to him and was on her knees leaning over Stan. She gently touched his head with trembling hands, then started feeling his chest.

It all hurt, but he didn't say anything.

"Can you breathe?" she asked him.

Stan tried taking a deep breath in through his mouth, and it made him start coughing.

The coughing actually hurt worse than getting kicked, but at least the air was getting back into his body, and he could breathe.

"I don't think anything is broken," his mom said miserably. "Where does it hurt?"

"I'm fine."

"Stan—"

"I'm *fine!*" he yelled, which made him start coughing again.

He pushed her away with arms that felt as weak as a baby's.

Stan didn't know why he was doing it. He wasn't mad at her. It wasn't her fault. But right then, he just felt like if he didn't get away, get out of the house, he was going to explode.

It hurt worse than anything yet, but he made himself stand, sliding his body up the broken wall. His mom was still talking to him, pleading with him, but Stan was done listening.

He half ran, half stumbled out of the house and into the dark.

Just another Friday night with the family, he thought, trying not to cry.

16

"Land isn't something you buy;
it's something you belong to."
—*GRANDPA JAMIE*

Elpidia wasn't paying full attention to the conversation happening a few feet away from her, but the bits she did hear were enough to tell her the old white lady who owned the motel wasn't ready for Abuela.

One of her grandmother's favorite things to do besides cooking and watching telenovelas was to argue with any kind of salesperson over the price of things. It didn't matter what the thing was: Elpidia's grandmother refused to pay whatever the seller was asking, at least not without doing and saying everything she could think of to get them to lower their price. Most of the time she convinced them to agree to let her pay what she wanted. If she couldn't convince them, Abuela would usually walk away and go somewhere else and try again.

A lot of times Elpidia had watched Abuela pretend not to speak English just to confuse a salesperson and get them to lose their patience. That was Elpidia's favorite. It always made her laugh. Not out loud, though. Her grandmother had warned her sternly more than once never to laugh while she was "negotiating."

Elpidia wasn't sure what Abuela was negotiating with the motel lady, or why they'd left the cantina in the middle of the day to have Tío Raymond drive them over here. She occupied herself by carefully walking around the ledge of an old, cracked water fountain that was missing as many little dingy white tiles as were still attached to it. There was no water inside the fountain either, just broken bottles and old take-out containers, a bunch of which looked like they might have come from their restaurant.

The motel was a good ten miles down the road from the cantina. It backed right up to the shore of the Salton Sea. The mountains beyond looked like giant tombstones huddled together in a graveyard.

It wasn't like any other motel Elpidia had seen in real life or even on TV. Each "room" was its own separate little building, all of them spaced out around each other randomly in no seeming pattern. Their roofs looked crooked, all slanting down to one side like ramps. Instead of a regular door, each one had a big sliding piece of glass in front. They looked like weird old box televisions to Elpidia.

Still, it was the only motel around for miles.

Abuela paced over to the dry fountain, the bottom of her cane crunching pebbly sand with each step. She settled herself on the ledge, leaning the cane between her knees and resting both hands on top of it.

"Ven aquí, mija," her grandmother called to her.

Elpidia quickly retraced her steps back around the fountain wall and dropped down to sit beside her.

"What do you think of this place?"

"What? The motel?" Elpidia shrugged. "It's fine. I guess. Why?"

"Your abuela is going to buy it, I think."

Elpidia stared at her like she'd just said she was going to board a rocket ship to the moon and open a taqueria in one of its craters.

"Buy it?" she asked in shock. "Why would you *want* it? This place is a hole."

"It's a good business, whatever it looks like. We'd only keep it open in the seasons when we get the tourists around here."

Elpidia never understood why *anyone* would come all the way out here, especially just for fun. It was cheap, she supposed, but there had to be other places to go camping and hiking that weren't hotter than the sun, didn't smell like dead fish, and weren't full of scorpions and snakes and lizards. Yet every spring and summer, the lake would be filled with fancy boats hauled down to the desert from far-away towns where the houses were bigger and richer than anything in the Estates. There was even an old sailing club on the far side of the Salton Sea that no one who actually lived in Lakeshore could afford to belong to.

"And I have some ideas," her grandmother went on. "Like maybe we get some of those four-wheeler things, the desert bikes, and the dune buggies. Rent them out to the summer gringos. Make 'em a deal if they rent the bikes and rooms here together."

"But how can you run the cantina and this place at the same time?"

"The family will help. Your tío Raymond is always talking about how he wants to be a businessman. And I've got you."

Elpidia blinked at her. "Me?"

Abuela nodded. "I'd be counting on you, too. And I'm thinking . . . maybe one day you can take over the cantina for me."

That idea made Elpidia feel like she was being split right down the middle of herself.

She loved cooking, and she loved the restaurant. More than that, it meant everything to her that Abuela would trust her one day with the thing she and her husband had built up from nothing. Elpidia knew her grandmother loved her, had always loved her, but since the fire Elpidia couldn't help feeling like she was a burden, as if her grandmother *had* to take her in after her parents were sent away and she didn't choose to do it on her own.

It made Elpidia feel good to know that wasn't true.

Still, she didn't want her life to be in the Estates, in the middle of this forgotten desert with its sad speckles of lonely houses next to a lake that smelled like death most of the time. As much as she loved Abuela and the restaurant, Elpidia wanted to use cooking to take her away from all of this.

She didn't know how to tell her grandmother any of that.

"You getting quiet on me now, mija?"

Elpidia was saved from having to come up with the words to answer her grandmother by the roar of a powerful engine thundering across the courtyard.

It was Grandpa Jamie on his big motorcycle. He rolled to a stop beside the office out front that was the size of hot dog stand.

The motel lady Abuela had been negotiating with popped her head out of the window, looking like she was ready to call the cops on the old biker.

Jamie just smiled at her as he turned off the engine and leaned his motorcycle on its kickstand.

He took his time climbing off the bike, and every time he moved, he grunted and cursed under his breath as if it was painful.

Elpidia was happy to see him again so soon, but she felt nervous too, like it meant something bad was going to happen. She looked at Abuela and thought she saw a slight frown on her grandmother's face.

"Afternoon, ladies," he said to them. "I went by the cantina, and that old busboy of yours told me you was out here. He was pretty gruff about it. I don't think he likes Indians."

"Flavio doesn't like anybody," Elpidia assured her grandfather.

Jamie smiled down at her.

"I bet he likes *you* just fine. You got a way about you, Little Squirrel. A strength. Like your daddy had."

"What is it you want, Jamie?" Abuela asked him.

Grandpa Jamie put his hands on his hips and stared above the strange little glass-doored cottages at the mountains in the distance.

"Been thinking about y'all since I saw you upstate. I was

remembering . . . that last cookout we was all at together, what was it? Two summers ago now? Yeah, I guess it was two summers. Better times."

Abuela didn't say anything.

Elpidia felt awkward because her grandmother didn't say anything.

"Anyway, I got a birthday coming up. This weekend the whole clan's going to be at my spread. I wanted to invite you and yours. We's still family, after all."

"Your birthday isn't until November, James," Abuela reminded him.

Grandpa Jamie laughed.

"Like I said, you never forget anything."

He sighed a big heavy breath.

"Close enough, ain't it? I just figure it's been too long since we was all together. I miss my granddaughter."

Abuela looked at Elpidia, who didn't know what to say.

"I understand," her grandmother said. "I would too. She can come if she wants to, but bringing the whole family . . . too many hotheads, James. Too much bad blood. On both sides."

"No such thing as bad blood," he insisted.

Elpidia watched her grandfather closely. He looked like he was hurting again, like when he climbed off his bike, but it was a different kind of pain he was feeling now.

"I'm seventy years old, Florentina. I've buried two wives. I got one boy in the ground, another on lockdown, another one in and out of jail, probably won't live to see his forties the way he goes on. I need all the family I can claim."

Elpidia swallowed hard. It wasn't easy hearing her grandfather talk like that. When he said he had a son in "lockdown," she knew he meant her dad. She also knew her dad had lost a brother when they were all very young, but no one ever really seemed to want to tell that story.

Grandpa Jamie's son who was "in and out of jail" and probably wouldn't live to see his forties was her uncle Desmond, who everyone called "Dez," her dad's older brother. He'd been in and out of trouble her whole life. He had a really bad temper.

"We share more than Little Squirrel here," Jamie went on. "Our families both go back a long ways. All this blame and anger ain't doing any of us any good. I'm just invitin' y'all to come eat. So come eat."

Elpidia looked at her grandmother, wanting to say something, but not feeling like she was allowed to.

She wanted to go, though. She missed her grandfather. He reminded her of her dad, and however mad Elpidia was at both her parents, she liked feeling like he was still there somehow.

As much as all of that, she wanted their families to get along again. She missed that as much as she missed her parents.

Abuela must've felt Elpidia's gaze because she turned her head slowly to look back at her.

Elpidia thought she saw the deep lines in her grandmother's face soften a bit.

"I'll bring Elpidia," Abuela finally gave in. "I'll tell everybody else, but I can't make anyone come who doesn't want to."

Grandpa Jamie smiled. He looked at Elpidia knowingly.

She smiled back. She knew what he was thinking because she was thinking the same thing.

When Abuela said she couldn't make anyone come, that was just her being humble. She could make anyone in their family do anything she wanted. Everyone respected her, and they were even more afraid of her.

Elpidia was pretty sure in that moment that her whole family would be at Grandpa Jamie's party.

17

"It doesn't matter if you're fighting
more than one, not if you're trained
and they're not. It takes a lot of numbers
to make up for skill."
—*CHARLIE*

It was turning into a rough weekend for Stan. He felt like
he couldn't go home after what happened. He'd slept at
school, curling up on one of the lunch tables and shivering
against the cold all night. He couldn't face his mom right
now. He was worried about her, and she was probably worried about him. Even though it wasn't the first time he'd
had to stay away from home all night on his own. He felt
like such a failure.

There was no way for him to get to Charlie's place,
either. Elpidia and her family weren't around. They'd

driven down to the border to visit Elpidia's uncle, who the government was trying to deport from the country. They'd even closed the cantina for the day. He didn't have anywhere else to go. He was alone.

It made his stomach hurt, thinking about that. It didn't used to be a big deal, him being alone. He was always alone. He thought he was used to it. He'd even told himself that he liked it that way.

That was all before his mother took him to Charlie for the first time and he'd met Elpidia. It was before they became friends. Because that's what they were, he realized. He hadn't really let himself think about it until now, not even while he was spending all the time hanging out with her. Maybe he'd been afraid to call her his friend because she wouldn't feel the same way, but he knew that wasn't true. He had his first real friend.

And he really needed her right now.

All Stan could do was wander around the Estates. He was hungry and thirsty, and his chest and head still hurt, but there was nothing to be done about any of it.

It was getting hot as he wandered down Dolphin Street, about four blocks from the burned-out remains of Elpidia's house. He didn't know why he was walking in that direction. Maybe it was just to feel connected to her while she was gone.

He really wished he had one of his books.

"Where you going, man?" someone to his right asked Stan.

Stan recognized the kid right away. He was an eighth grader at Stan's school, one of the Los Cocos who'd been at the cantina with Mezco. His name was Hector. Everyone at their school knew that name. Hector had a reputation for twisting arms and necks until you gave him whatever you had in your pockets. Stan had never made him work that hard, though.

He'd just walked out of the desert and onto the street where Stan was idling.

"Nowhere," Stan said.

"What you got in your pockets?"

That was a different voice, coming from behind Stan. He hadn't even known anyone else was there. He turned around and saw another one of the gang members he recognized from Abuela's place, younger than Hector. He'd been in Stan's class for a while, in fact, but just stopped coming one day. He couldn't remember the kid's name, though.

"Nothing," Stan told him.

"Let us see," Hector insisted.

Stan frowned. "No."

"Let me see or I'm about to jack you up," Hector threatened him.

The older boy didn't wait for Stan to answer him this time, though. He rushed at Stan, his arm raised and his fist cocked to throw a punch.

Stan felt his body tense and his hands leave his pockets where they'd been stuffed. It was like alarms were going off inside his head. He didn't want to get hit again. He was in enough pain.

But he didn't freeze like he had at home the night before. Something had changed in him. He wasn't afraid of these guys like he would've been before, and he didn't overthink or worry or panic about every bad thing they could say or do to him.

Neither of them was his father.

Stan swept his right leg back and to the side, turning his body in the same direction and dodging the punch altogether. Hector threw the punch so hard that when he missed, he went sailing past Stan and stumbling across the pavement, almost falling down.

The older boy managed to stay on his feet, though. He turned back to Stan and swung again. This time Stan did exactly what Charlie had taught him to do. He blocked the shot with his left hand, pushing Hector's wrist away, and at the same time with his other hand he punched Hector right in the nose, connecting perfectly. His body even remembered to push off from his foot and twist his hip into it to give the shot as much power as Stan could muster. He felt Hector's nose crunch under his fist.

Hector staggered back a few steps and bent over at the waist, holding both hands over his nose and saying some really bad words.

Stan couldn't believe it. He watched Hector with wide, stunned eyes. He was still in shock when the other kid landed a punch right into the side of his head out of nowhere. Stan felt it, but he'd been hit before plenty of times and a lot harder than that by someone way bigger. All it did was let him know that there was more danger and where that danger was standing.

Like he'd done a moment ago, Stan just reacted. He didn't think about it. He launched an elbow right into the kid's cheek, pushing him with the hand of his other arm as he did. The kid was smaller than Stan, and he went flying, landing hard on the street.

Stan had dropped him, all right, but it gave Hector enough time to recover from the shock and sting of his bloody nose and the tears it brought to his eyes. Yelling through his teeth, he ran at Stan and tried to tackle him like a football player.

Hector might've been older and taller, but Stan was twice the size of an ordinary sixth grader and very hard to move. He didn't fall over when Hector grabbed him.

Instead, the two started wrestling with each other on their feet. Stan and Elpidia hadn't done much grappling with Charlie. They'd mostly worked with sticks and on strikes and defense.

So, Stan went on instinct. He tried to keep Hector's arms tied up with his so that the eighth grader couldn't hit him or get a good hold on Stan. At the same time, Stan wrapped one of his legs around Hector's and leaned all his weight forward, tripping him and making him fall backward with Stan on top of him.

He heard Hector groan and felt Hector's body tense up when they hit the ground. Hector stopped breathing for a second, and with Stan on top of him, he couldn't get his wind back.

Stan finally rolled off him, feeling like it was safe and that Hector wasn't going to be able to do anything, for a minute at least.

Lying there in the middle of the street, Stan's head fell to one side, and through blurry eyes, he saw a pair of white socks pulled high up to someone's knees.

"That's enough, yo!" the owner of the socks barked like a mad pit bull.

Stan sat up slowly, blinking away some sweat that was collecting in his eyes.

He found himself staring up at Mezco.

Stan scrambled quickly to get back to his feet.

"What did I do?" he asked frantically.

His hands were raised, and his feet were planted to continue the fight, even against Mezco.

Behind him, the younger boy was helping Hector get back up, but Hector pushed him away so he could stand on his own.

The gang leader only laughed at Stan, though.

"Relax, yo, you didn't do nothin'. This was like . . . what do you call it? What actors do? An audition! This was just an audition. I needed to see if all those skills Charlie has been passing on worked."

Stan looked over at Hector and the other boy. They were just standing there, both of them still breathing hard from the fight. Hector seemed mad about his nose, but he wasn't looking at Stan like he was mad at *him*.

"So you were just . . . you were, like, testing me?"

"And you get a gold star," Mezco told him. "Those were some dope moves. You're not just big—you're fast."

"For a white boy," Hector admitted, spitting blood onto the street.

Stan had never thought *anything* about him was fast.

"Did my boys do that?" Mezco asked.

Stan wasn't sure what he meant.

The Los Cocos leader pointed at Stan's chest.

Stan looked down at himself. The collar of his shirt had been yanked and stretched during the fight, and you could see his bare chest. There was a huge purple-and-blue bruise right in the middle of it where his father had punted Stan like a football.

"No," Stan said quietly. "That was, uh . . . it was somebody else."

"Oh yeah?"

Stan just nodded.

Mezco walked over to him and gently slipped his arm around Stan's shoulders, leaning into him closely. His hand squeezed the top of Stan's arm.

"See, this is what I'm talking about," Mezco said to Stan, almost whispering in his ear. "If you've got problems, and you roll with Los Cocos, then those are *our* problems, too. And we'll take care of that business together. ¿Entiendes? You hear? It don't matter *who* it is. *Nobody* messes with you when you're one of us. *No one.*"

Mezco was asking Stan if he understood, but Stan didn't.

"Are you . . . do you mean, like, you want me to join your gang?"

It seemed impossible to Stan. This whole thing—the fight he'd just had, Mezco talking to him like this—seemed like some kind of weird dream he was having.

"I know talent when I see it," Mezco said. "And I could teach you a lot more than Charlie can. Think of it like graduating."

Mezco clapped his hand against Stan's arm, and then he let go of him, stepping back.

"You need a ride somewhere, Big Boy?"

Stan thought about it. He was thinking about a lot of things, like what Mezco had just said about helping Stan handle his "problem."

And the picture in Stan's head of Mezco and his gang all piling on top of Stan's father and beating him up made Stan feel good inside.

"No, I'm okay," Stan told him. "I'm just gonna walk home."

"We'll catch up with you later, then," Mezco promised.

He waved to his boys, and the three of them disappeared back into the desert where they'd come from.

Stan watched them go, rubbing the side of his head where the smaller Los Cocos member had popped him. It didn't really hurt, though.

Nothing hurt too bad right then.

Stan was too amped up to feel pain.

18

"Who you are isn't in your blood.
What's in your blood is an idea,
like something whispered to you from
the past. You have to decide what
to do with that."
—*GRANDPA JAMIE*

The bowl was large and heavy. Elpidia needed both arms to carry it against her chest. It was also still hot. She'd started marinating the pork the day before in adobada, a sauce Abuela showed her how to make from several kinds of dried peppers, garlic, vinegar, and oregano, but Elpidia cooked it fresh that morning to bring to Grandpa Jamie's "birthday" party. There were also several dozen corn tortillas she'd helped roll out and fry up to go with them.

Her grandfather had a modest house on a couple acres of dirt and patchy grass two hours east of Lakeshore Estates, far enough away from the Salton Sea for Elpidia to forget about it. The yard around his house was buzzing by the time they got there. There were dozens of people drinking and eating and hollering, little kids running around chasing each other, along with a whole pack of dogs that were probably as much strays as actually belonged to Jamie.

Just as Elpidia had suspected, Abuela made pretty much all her relatives come along. There were four cars' worth of them, Elpidia's cousins and uncles and aunts. Even Flavio the busboy, who was barely family if he even was related to them by blood, had been forced to abandon his apron and tub sink for the day. Abuela had gone so far as to close the cantina.

Elpidia hadn't talked to everyone, but she'd heard a lot of whining and cursing when they all piled into their cars to caravan over. Tío Raymond complained the entire way. He only stopped when they finally arrived and got out of the car.

Elpidia was happy to be free of him, of all of them.

There were three long folding tables set up in the shape of a "U" and draped with faded tablecloths. Every table was filled with food. Nearby there was a whole little village of coolers of every color all sitting on the ground, filled with ice and sodas and water, and beers for the adults.

Elpidia remembered going to a big Cahuilla festival

once where they celebrated the agave harvest. Agave was a plant they use to make things like medicine and tequila, both of which Elpidia had only ever smelled, and they smelled horrible. At the festival, they cut off leaves from the agave plant, roasted them over hot coals, and passed them around to everybody to eat. Elpidia thought they tasted like fruity cough syrup.

She remembered Grandpa Jamie agreeing with her and telling her they only did it for the festival. Elpidia was glad to see the food at his party was different. There were some of the same things she'd had at the festival, but it was all the good stuff, like bowls of smoky beans, pots of what smelled like rabbit stew, purees made from acorn, fry bread, and all kinds of cakes and pies.

As Elpidia carefully arranged her bowl of adobada pork among the other offerings, she looked across the yard and saw Grandpa Jamie standing with several other Native men. They were laughing as they took turns throwing wicked-looking knives at a target nailed to an old dead tree.

One of the men was her uncle Dez, her dad's brother. She recognized his clean-shaven head and the tattoo on the right side of his neck. It was a snake coiled into three circles. That tattoo had always scared her, ever since she was small.

"Little Squirrel!" Grandpa Jamie called to her from across the patchy dirt field.

He put his knife away in a holster that was hanging from his belt down his right hip.

Elpidia watched him jog over to her at the food tables, making funny faces at her as if running, even really slow like that, was killing him.

It made her laugh.

"Did I see you carrying a big ol' bowl of something good?"

Elpidia nodded proudly. "Adobada. It's pork. I remember you liked mom's pork."

"Is it spicy?"

Elpidia pinched her fingers close together and held them up in front of her right eye, grinning at him.

Grandpa Jamie laughed and hugged her with one arm.

"I'm glad you came, Granddaughter."

She hugged him back, suddenly feeling too emotional to speak.

"I'll try some of that pork. I can handle a little spicy."

She faked punching him in the stomach.

"You act a lot older than you feel," she said.

He laughed again. "You're like your grandma. You see too much."

As they were talking, Uncle Dez walked up beside her

grandfather. He was drinking from a large plastic bottle of orange juice that was only half full.

Elpidia wondered what else was in the bottle besides orange juice.

Dez gave her a long, appraising look up and down.

"You look like your daddy," he said, taking another swig and making a face that told her it definitely wasn't just juice he was drinking.

"Your brother ain't that pretty," Grandpa Jamie told him.

Dez snorted.

"That punk Raymond come with y'all?" he asked her.

"He drove us."

"Never liked that kid."

Grandpa Jamie reached up and grasped Dez by the back of his neck.

"What did we talk about for today, huh? Keeping cool, no?"

Her uncle Dez knocked away Jamie's hand, but he didn't talk back to his father.

"Go play with your cousins, Little Squirrel," Jamie said to her. "I'm going to go pay my respects to the rest of your kin."

He practically dragged her uncle Dez away.

Elpidia wanted to tell him not to go. She didn't want

to be on her own. But she couldn't say that to her grand-father.

She stayed there by the food for a while, watching the people who came to make plates with a little of everything on them. Some she didn't recognize, friends of Jamie's, probably. Some of the folks she did know, and they even said hello to her and asked about how her parents were holding up. Elpidia just tried to smile, and she'd say they were fine, even though she didn't really know.

It didn't take long for the party to break into two dif-ferent groups, she noticed. All of the people who'd come with her and Abuela had formed their own circles on the edge of the yard and weren't talking much to any of the Native guests. She watched her grandfather make his way from Abuela to the rest, doing his best to be friendly and welcoming and trying to make everybody laugh.

After a while, Elpidia looked over and noticed Mari-gold. She was sitting by herself on top of one of the coolers. It was the first time she'd ever seen Marigold alone with-out their little cousins all swarming around her.

She felt a quick rush of fear run through her, like they were back on the schoolyard. Elpidia shook that off, though. Marigold wasn't gunning for her here. The older girl looked different than she did at school. She looked almost sad.

Elpidia took a long, deep breath and let it out. Her first thought was to just leave it alone, but then she remembered that they'd all come here to try to make things better, like they were before.

Elpidia decided she had to do her part, whatever happened.

She walked over to the coolers, arms folded nervously across her chest, and quietly sat down on one of the big cold chests near Marigold.

"Hey."

Marigold looked over. Her face didn't really change. She didn't say anything right away, either.

At least it didn't look like she wanted to hurt Elpidia.

"I made stuff for tacos if you want," she offered. "I could make us plates."

"I'm not hungry," Marigold said.

"Okay."

Elpidia wasn't sure what else to say. She thought maybe asking Marigold questions might help.

"How come you're sitting here by yourself?"

Marigold shrugged. "I just . . . needed a break. I always have to watch those little snots, my sisters and our cousins. It's, like, my job because I'm the oldest. This is the only time off I get, when they can run around at one of these things."

Elpidia nodded. She'd always thought of them as Marigold's "gang." It never occurred to Elpidia they were Marigold's responsibility, whether her cousin wanted it or not.

She thought the older girl was done talking, but then Marigold really surprised her.

"You know, I used to . . . sometimes I'd go to see your mom when I had a problem."

"I didn't know that."

"Yeah, well, that was before she and your dad started doing . . . you know, whatever. She stopped listening after that. Or I guess she stopped being able to listen."

"Yeah, I know," Elpidia said tightly, trying hard not to remember all the times she said things to her mom and it felt like talking to a ghost.

"But before that," Marigold went on, "she was always . . . she'd help me. She'd try, anyway. I never had anyone one else to talk to, or at least anyone who listened or cared. She was a good auntie. It really sucked when they took her away."

Elpidia thought for a second Marigold was going to cry, but her cousin just swallowed back whatever was rising through her throat.

"You're mad she left you," Elpidia said.

She didn't say it like a question because Elpidia could

see in Marigold's face and hear in her words that it was true.

"Yeah," her cousin admitted. "I guess I am."

"I'm mad, too. At both of them. But, y'know, at least they didn't torch all of *your* stuff."

That made Marigold laugh. She put her hands over her mouth, like she was embarrassed.

"Sorry, I shouldn't laugh at that."

Elpidia shrugged. "It's okay. You have to laugh, I think. Or else you just start crying. I don't know why those are the only choices, but that's how it feels."

Marigold nodded, looking like she agreed with Elpidia's words.

"I was mad at you, too," Marigold said a while later.

Elpidia was surprised. "Why? What did I do?"

"You didn't *do* anything. You just . . . you had your other family to go to, at least. Your mom's family. Your grandma. I don't have anybody. My mom ran off . . . who knows where. My dad has half a brain on his best days. My cousins are littler than me, and they all look up to me for answers and stuff."

"I'm sorry," Elpidia said, and she really meant it. "I didn't think about any of that. I just thought you were being a jerk."

They both laughed.

It felt good, laughing with her cousin instead of yelling and fighting with her.

"So, what, are we, like . . . cool now?" Elpidia asked when they were done laughing.

"You said you wanted to squash it, right? And Grandfather told everyone before you all got here that we needed to be chill. So, this is me being chill."

"But what about school?"

"We'll just leave each other alone, I guess."

Elpidia nodded. "Or . . . we could hang out. Stan and me hold down a good shade tree. I'll bring food for everybody."

Marigold smiled a little at that.

"Your boy can take a punch," she said. "He stood tall for you. That's a good friend, right there."

"Yeah. He is good."

Elpidia was about to ask about Marigold's favorite foods, thinking she could maybe cook something for her, when they heard raised voices shouting across their grandfather's backyard, angry voices smashing into each other and saying curses the kids weren't allowed to say.

Elpidia and Marigold both stood up from the coolers and walked toward the commotion.

Something had finally brought Abuela's side and Jamie's side together. They were lining up around Dez and

Raymond, who were squaring off and getting right in each other's face. Raymond was smaller than Desmond, but he was also cocky, and he didn't want to back down from anyone.

"Dezzy is always startin' something," Marigold muttered under her breath, shaking her head.

"What's his problem with Raymond?"

"I dunno. He's better-looking? He's never been to jail? Has all his teeth? Take your pick."

Elpidia wanted to laugh, but there were too many nerves making her stomach and her head bubble and spin.

This was exactly what she *didn't* want to happen.

She kept waiting for someone to step between them and squash it. Elpidia's eyes searched frantically for Grandpa Jamie, the one person she knew Uncle Dez would listen to, or Abuela, the one person she knew Tío Raymond would listen to. She couldn't spot either of them.

Without anybody to calm the situation, it wasn't long before Dez said something that crossed a line for Raymond. She didn't hear what it was, but she saw her tío's eyes widen, and in the next moment he threw a punch right into the side of Desmond's head.

It was on after that. The two of them started swinging wildly at each other. It wasn't like a fight in a movie. It was messy and chaotic and ugly, and they were both so angry and out of control. It was a scary thing to watch.

But it didn't stop with Dez and Raymond throwing hands. Instead of breaking up the fight, the other cousins and uncles and friends surrounding the two of them started shoving each other and arguing. The pushing and shouting turned into more hands being thrown, and in what felt like the blink of her eyes, the entire party looked like they were fighting each other with punches and kicks.

Elpidia looked nervously up at Marigold.

"Does this mean we have to start fighting, too?" she asked.

Marigold shook her head.

"I'd rather do those tacos," she said.

The rest of the kids all huddled off to the side of the sudden battle, being herded together by moms and aunties to keep them away from the fighting.

Dez and Raymond wrestled with each other across the yard, still standing on their feet. It almost looked like they were dancing. The thought caused Elpidia to giggle nervously, even though she didn't think anything else about what was happening was funny.

Her giggling died when Dez and Raymond finally ended up crashing through the food table at the bottom of the "U" shape, snapping every leg of the table and sending the entire spread of offerings atop it across the yard.

"My adobada!" Elpidia yelled at them angrily.

Just when Elpidia felt like she was about to start crying,

the crack of what sounded like thunder filled her ears.

It wasn't just her. The sound was so loud and sudden that it made most of her family members doing the fighting pause mid-punch like they were in a video game or something.

Even Dez and Raymond stopped going at it to see what was happening.

She and Marigold looked over to see Grandpa Jamie standing next to Abuela, who was leaning heavily on her cane with both hands.

Their grandfather was holding a shotgun that looked half as tall as Elpidia herself. The end of it was still smoking from Grandpa Jamie shooting it into the air above them.

The whole backyard was quiet. Everyone was looking at the oldest members of both families.

"Y'all get it out of your systems now?" Grandpa Jamie asked no one in particular, speaking to the family as a whole.

No one answered him, at least not out loud. But slowly, one by one, they all backed away from whoever they'd been wrestling or throwing hands with. There was no more angry yelling or cursing, except from a few of the aunties who were chastising their men.

Uncle Dez was the only one who didn't seem to want the fight to be over.

Grandpa Jamie set the butt of his shotgun on the

ground and leaned it toward Abuela, who held it for him like it was a second cane.

Elpidia watched her grandfather stalk over to where Dez and Raymond were still lying in all the smeared and smashed food, a lot of it covering their clothes. Jamie reached down and grabbed a handful of Desmond's collar, hauling him up to his feet whether the younger man wanted to go or not.

She was surprised by how strong Jamie looked in that moment, how much power and authority he still had in him. Seventy years old or not, he was still in charge.

"Is this how you chill?" he growled at his son. "Is this how you respect your kin?"

"They ain't my kin!" Dez yelled at his father, snot bubbling from his nose and cake covering his bald head. "They ain't never gonna be my kin! *Her* neither!"

Elpidia's eyes widened as she realized he was talking about her.

Uncle Dez kept on wriggling like a fish Jamie had pulled from a river, spitting and cursing and pushing against him.

Her grandfather finally had enough. He slapped Desmond right across his jaw. It wasn't a light slap, either. It sounded like the thud of something heavy being dropped on the ground.

Dez stopped struggling. He looked stunned. Elpidia couldn't tell if it was because Jamie half knocked him out with the slap or if Dez was just surprised. It might have been both.

Grandpa Jamie gripped Desmond even tighter by his collar and practically threw him across the yard. Dez went stumbling, almost tripping over his own feet, but he managed to stay upright.

"Go in the house or get on your bike and take off," Jamie ordered him. "It's your choice. But don't be where I can see you for a while, ya hear?"

Desmond looked back at his father, his shoulders rising and falling rapidly, and his chest doing the same from how hard he was still breathing.

He didn't look mad to Elpidia anymore. He looked sad, like his feelings were hurt.

She almost felt bad for him, but her feelings were still hurt, too.

Dez didn't go into the house. Instead he turned and ran around it, out to the front. A few seconds later, she could hear the sound of a motorcycle engine, and they all watched him ride away.

Grandpa Jamie walked over to Abuela and picked up his shotgun. He carried it back inside his house without saying another word.

"I better see *everyone* helping clean up!" Abuela shouted across the yard. "And I mean right now!"

She yelled some more stuff in Spanish that was just for her family, and none of it was good.

Everybody started moving. Raymond climbed out of the mess he and Dez had made and tried to wipe himself off.

Abuela just watched him and shook her head like she was ashamed of him.

Elpidia felt a hand on her shoulder, and it surprised her enough that she jumped a little.

But it was only Marigold, looking at her with a sympathy in her eyes Elpidia hadn't seen before.

"You okay?" her cousin asked.

She nodded.

"That wasn't cool, what he said," Marigold told her. "He didn't mean it, anyway. I've heard him say a lot worse about all of us when he's like that. Don't worry about it, okay?"

Elpidia didn't know why, and if she'd stopped to think about it, she would've been too embarrassed to do it, but she put her arms around Marigold and hugged her.

She could feel her cousin tense up, like she was surprised, but after a second Marigold hugged her back.

It really helped. Elpidia couldn't believe how much it helped her in that moment.

The sun was starting to set, and somehow the rest of the night turned out to be a lot like that hug. It was as if having the big brawl, and especially watching Dez act so bitterly and speak so angrily in front of everybody, had made them see all see how wild and ignorant they were behaving toward each other.

After the mess was cleaned up, everybody started eating what was left of the food and drinking and talking and laughing. It stopped being two different groups, and everyone mixed in with everyone else, just like it used to be.

Grandpa Jamie lit a bunch of torches that were supposed to keep the bugs away, and a few people who'd brought guitars broke them out and started playing. The others at the party gathered around them to sing. They sang bolero songs in Spanish. They sang Cahuilla songs. They sang country songs in English. When people didn't know the words, they just clapped along and enjoyed it.

After a while, Elpidia saw her grandfather smile again. What happened with Desmond had really seemed to upset him.

In between songs, Elpidia went over to him and brought him a can of beer.

"Thank you, Granddaughter," he said, taking it and popping the lid.

"I'm sorry you had to throw Uncle Dez out," she said.

Grandpa Jamie waved the thought away with his hand.

"Don't you worry about that, Little Squirrel. It wasn't the first time. Won't be the last. And it's not your fault, neither. Your daddy'd beat Dezzie's butt if he'd heard what Dez said about you. And he'd be right to do it, too. Don't you pay it no mind."

He reached out and gently squeezed her shoulder, looking into Elpidia's eyes.

"You're always welcome here. You remember that."

"Thank you, Grandpa," she said quietly, feeling like if she tried to speak any louder, the words would break apart.

He nodded, patting her shoulder and giving her a smile and a wink.

"Good, then. Glad that's settled."

Abuela had eased into a lawn chair, holding her cane between her knees and tapping the bottom of it against the dirt in rhythm with the music being played.

Elpidia walked over to her and hunkered down beside her chair.

"Are you glad we came?" she asked her grandmother.

The expression on Abuela's face didn't change.

"Are you?"

Elpidia nodded enthusiastically.

Her grandmother smiled, if only just a little.

"That's all that matters, then. They're your blood, at the end of the day."

"Do you think everybody will still be cool with each

other after today? Do you think this'll last?"

Her grandmother sighed, not answering her right away.

Finally, she said, "Family is the only thing that does last, mija."

Elpidia wasn't sure that meant "yes," but she didn't think it meant "no," either, at least not a for sure "no."

She decided that was enough for now.

19

"It don't matter where they went.
They don't live here anymore."
—*MEZCO*

Stan realized it was the first time he'd actually seen Charlie leave his compound in the deep desert since Charlie started training him and Elpidia. He'd begun to think of Charlie like a monk from a movie or one of Stan's novels, and that barbed-wire-fenced spread of Charlie's was like his monastery, a holy temple where he spent his life thinking about whatever holy men thought about all the time.

Stan sat in the cab of one of the old pickup trucks from Charlie's yard. He was surprised any of Charlie's cars actually ran. He thought Charlie just collected them as decoration, or maybe to sell them for scrap metal. They were driving out toward the edge of the Estates, where you went from seeing a few houses on every other street to seeing no houses at all.

He'd called Charlie because Stan didn't know what else to do, or who else to talk to about Mezco and Los Cocos who would understand. Elpidia would have listened, but he hadn't seen her at school because Stan had been cutting school, not wanting anyone to make him go back home. And now she was away with the rest of her family attending her grandfather's big party. Charlie had given Stan's mom his cell phone number to work out the schedule with Stan's training.

As soon as Stan told Charlie what happened, about his "audition," Charlie insisted on coming to pick Stan up so they could "deal with it," or at least that's what Charlie said.

He'd never seen or heard Charlie act like this before, almost like he was scared. Normally Charlie was the most chill person Stan had ever met. Nothing bothered him. Nothing made him nervous or excited. He just walked his slow walk and smiled his little smile, never in a hurry and never disturbed.

Because of that, it was extra weird and upsetting seeing

Charlie like this. He wasn't smiling, and he was driving fast.

"Why didn't you just tell him no?" he asked Stan.

"You mean Mezco?"

"Yeah."

"Everything happened really fast. I didn't know what to say."

"You should've said 'no.'"

"Are you mad at me?"

Charlie sighed. "No. It's not your fault. It's just . . ."

"What?" Stan pressed him.

Charlie shook his head. "Nothing. We'll take care of it."

Stan wasn't sure he should say anymore, but he couldn't help it. It had been on his mind since it happened.

"They said they could help me with . . . some problems at home."

Charlie took his eyes off the road for a minute to look at Stan seriously.

"I thought that's what I was doing."

That made Stan go quiet and still. He hadn't told Charlie about what happened before Stan ran into Mezco and his boys, with his father kicking him into the wall. He couldn't tell Charlie about how he froze up. He couldn't admit that after all Charlie had taught him, Stan had failed.

"Don't take what looks like the easy way out, Stanny," Charlie said, his voice heavier and more serious than Stan had ever heard him sound before. "And don't let people use you. I'm only telling you that because I've done both in my life, too many times. I don't want you to end up like me."

That was hard for Stan to hear, mostly because he wanted to think of Charlie as one of the coolest people he'd ever met. But for everything cool about him, for all he knew about fighting and surviving and hunting scorpions, Stan knew what Charlie meant. He didn't want Stan to grow up to be some guy living like a lonely ghost deep in the desert, doing deals with people like Mezco.

Stan also thought about what Elpidia told him on the bus, about why Mezco would want Stan in Los Cocos. That was what Charlie meant by letting people use him, whether it was for being so big for his age, or knowing how to fight, or especially because he looked like the people who were in charge in the Estates.

That wasn't right, and it wasn't fair, and Stan didn't want to be part of it.

He didn't realize where they were going until they were almost there. He knew about the ruins of the old stone house. His mom and his father had even driven him out here to explore it once a long time ago when Stan could barely walk. That was back before the old man started drinking every single day and stopped working.

He didn't want to think about them right now, especially his mom. Stan felt like he'd abandoned her by not going back home yet. He felt guilty and ashamed. At the same time, he was also mad at her for keeping them in that house all these years with his father. It didn't make any sense, how he could feel sorry *and* angry.

Maybe it was because he knew, adult or not, his mom felt just as trapped as he did.

The stone house was in the middle of the desert, way off the road. At least it used to be a house, a long time ago. It had been made entirely out of rocks, and no one really knew by who. It was before Lakeshore Estates existed, maybe back in the old days when the first settlers had made it this far west into the desert.

Whoever built it, the house had either collapsed or fallen apart over time. Now there were just rocks everywhere, small pieces and big pieces. Some little sections of the walls still stood, so you could tell how big the house was and the shape of it. But the only part of the house that had really survived was the chimney. It shot up from the sand a good twenty or thirty feet into the air, this big column of rocks. And on the back of the chimney were steps, like an old staircase that led to a second floor or an attic that didn't exist anymore.

They were just steps to nowhere now.

Off from where the remains of the crumbled house were spread over the sand, there was an old wooden shack that leaned so crooked and so far to one side it looked like it should have fallen down a long time ago. Charlie called it a smokehouse and said it's where people would store meat before there were any kind of refrigerators or electricity.

Next to the smokehouse, a dozen dirt bikes and motorcycles were lined up, all of them leaning against their kickstands.

Charlie turned off the road, and they bounced up and down in their seats for a few minutes until he parked the truck near the bikes.

It looked like Los Cocos had made the ruins their own private hangout. They were all sitting on the old rocks, some of them drinking from bottles with paper bags wrapped around them, talking and laughing. There were girls there, too. It looked like a party.

"Come on," Charlie said.

Stan looked at him, feeling his stomach start to knot again.

"Are you sure?"

"It'll be okay," Charlie told him.

They climbed down from the truck's cab, and Stan

followed him across the sand over to where the ruins started.

"Yo, what's up!" Mezco shouted down to them from the very top of the staircase.

Stan saw he was standing on the top step with his arm around a very pretty girl.

"This is Big Boy! This is the vato I told you all about! ¡Muy fuerte! ¡Mucho corazón!"

The rest of Los Cocos, and even their girlfriends, started cheering for Stan.

It surprised him. He'd never had anyone cheer for him before.

"Mez," Charlie called up to the leader of Los Cocos. "Let me holler at you."

"Yeah, hold on a minute," Mezco said.

He kissed the girl he was with on the cheek and whispered something in her ear that made her giggle.

Mezco walked back down the old stone steps until he got to the middle, then he jumped from the column all the way to the ground, landing on his feet.

He walked over to meet them, slapping hands with Charlie and bumping fists the way they did.

"What's up?" Mezco asked. "To what do we owe this honor?"

"The kid is telling me y'all jumped him in," Charlie began.

"Nah, that was just a test. And he got *all* the gold stars."

Charlie leaned in close to Mezco. It seemed to Stan like it was really important to Charlie that only Mezco heard what Charlie had to say.

"Look, your business is your business. You know I respect you. I'm not here trying to tell you what to do. But the kid here . . . he's not about this game. This life ain't for him. So let's leave him out."

Mezco cocked his bald head to one side, staring at Charlie with a weird, confused-looking smile.

Then he started laughing, loud and long, and looking back at the other gang members, who started laughing along with him.

"You on some kind of dad trip, *Carlito*?" he asked Charlie with what Stan thought was a scary kind of grin.

Stan knew "Carlos" was Spanish for "Charles," and so "Carlito" must've been like a nickname.

"The kid's mom trusts me to look out for him," Charlie said.

Stan really didn't like how he kept calling him "kid," but he knew he shouldn't make a thing out of it in front of Mezco.

"She *pays* you to, you mean," Mezco corrected Charlie.

"It's my job either way."

Mezco shook his head. "It's your side hustle, Carlito.

We know what your job is. We got a good thing going, Charlie. Don't let this dad trip of yours get in the way of business."

Stan wondered what Mezco meant by that, what "business" he did with Charlie.

"You know, this really makes me sad, man, hearing you talk like this. Because I was making some big plans for us. I got the idea seeing what you done for Big Boy here. I was thinking you could start training *all* my soldiers. Teach 'em all that John Wick madness you been teaching these little niños. I thought it was a good idea. It made me feel all smart for coming up with it."

"We can talk about whatever," Charlie assured him, but Stan thought he sounded impatient and annoyed. "I just want to leave the kid out, that's all. I'm not telling you. I'm asking you."

"What about him? You ask him?"

Mezco nodded at Stan.

Charlie didn't answer. Instead, he looked down at Stan, waiting.

Stan understood it was on him to answer the question.

He kept thinking about the way Mezco put his arm around him and told him his problems would be Los Cocos' problems. Then he thought about all of them cheering for him just then, and how Mezco called him

"Big Boy." It always bothered Stan when people did that, especially people who just met him. They'd call him "Big Guy" or "Big Man" or whatever. He hated it. Except he didn't mind when Mezco called him that. He felt like the older boy was giving him respect.

Finally, though, Stan thought about Elpidia's grand-mother. He remembered when Mezco had thanked Abuela in her cantina for helping them with the sheriff, the way Abuela had said she was disappointed in Mezco and the other members of Los Cocos.

"I think I need to handle my own problems," Stan said.

Now it was Mezco who looked disappointed.

"Oh, so it's like that?" he asked Stan.

Stan nodded.

The look on Mezco's faced changed then. There was no more smiling or laughing or chill there.

In that moment, he reminded Stan a lot of his father.

"You come to my home to break me off some disre-spect like this?" Mezco asked, but even Stan understood he wasn't looking for an answer.

He was telling them.

"It's not like that," Charlie said.

The mood of the whole gang throughout the ruins changed in a second. Everyone who was sitting or lying down stood up. The ones who were talking with girls suddenly ignored them. All their attention turned to Charlie and Stan.

Mezco quickly raised an arm and snapped his fingers back at the rest of the gang.

"Everybody be chill," he ordered them.

No one did anything, but nobody sat back down, either. They kept staring at the intruders.

"Business, Carlito," Mezco said to Charlie. "Always business. I don't want to mess up ours. So take off now. Take Big Boy with you if you want. If he wants. But don't come back here unless you're ready to squab with me."

Charlie put a hand on Stan's shoulder, gently pulling him back.

"Let's go," he said.

Stan nodded, following Charlie as he walked them away from the ruins.

"Oye, Big Boy!" Mezco called to Stan, placing a hand to his chest. "You make me sad. In my heart. I had big plans for you. You're gonna be sorry!"

They climbed back into Charlie's truck. Stan was quick to close and lock his door.

He didn't say anything until they were back on the road driving far away from the old stone house.

"Do you . . . do you think . . . is it going to be okay?"

"I don't know, Stan," Charlie said. "I hope so. Either way, you're better off."

Stan wasn't sure how he meant that, but he didn't like the sound of it.

"What business do you do with them?" he asked.

Charlie didn't answer right away.

"I'm kind of like Elpidia. I'm a cook. I cook things for them. They sell what I make."

Stan frowned. "You're not talking about food though, are you?"

Charlie shook his head.

"So . . . why is it okay for you to do that, but you don't want me to roll with them?"

Charlie thought about that for a second before answering. When he spoke, it almost sounded like the words hurt him to say.

"Because you're better than me. You and Elpidia. You're good. You're good kids. And teaching you . . . is the only good thing I do. It's the last good thing I have. I didn't think I had any good things left for me. So, they can't have that. They can't have you. That's all."

Stan wasn't sure he understood, not all of it. What he did understand was that he was never going to know everything about Charlie, where he'd been or what he'd done in the past. He knew stuff had happened to him, though.

Bad stuff. And maybe he'd done bad stuff himself.

It probably should have made Stan see him differently, but it didn't. Charlie was still his teacher, and whatever else he'd done before Stan met him, he'd given Stan more than anyone ever had. Stan never would've become friends with Elpidia without Charlie.

He was glad he'd chosen him over Mezco, whatever happened because of it.

Stan just hoped nothing was going to happen.

20

"Everybody heals different, some faster,
some slower. Healing is one of those
things you can't rush, doesn't matter
what kind of injury it is."
—*CHARLIE*

Elpidia was worried about Stan. She hadn't seen him all week. He hadn't been at school, either. She would have gone to his house, but he'd told her never to do that because of his father, and the way he looked when he said it convinced Elpidia that he meant it.

Like she did every day, Elpidia walked from the bus stop, across the train tracks and the entrance to Lakeshore Estates, to the cantina to help prepare for the dinner rush that came around 6:00 p.m. every evening. She had potatoes to peel and boil, and queso fresco to make. Abuela had said they were even going to make Elpidia's ceviche a happy hour special, and she was excited.

The cantina wasn't even half full, being right between when things got busy for lunch and then again for dinner. There were a few regulars at the bar, locals from the Estates who *always* seemed to be there, hunched over the same drink, telling the same sad stories to Gabbi, their bartender who was never interested in hearing them for the hundredth time.

Elpidia waved to Gabbi as she walked into the kitchen and grabbed her apron from where it hung on a hook near the door. As she tied it on, she noticed Abuela wasn't there. She hadn't just gone to the bathroom or something, either. Her cane was gone from its usual spot. That was weird. Her grandmother was usually *always* in the kitchen this time of the day.

Instead, she found Flavio. He wasn't washing dishes and silverware in the big sink, either. He was slowly stirring a large pot of what smelled to Elpidia like pozole, her second favorite soup.

"Since when do you cook?" she asked the career busboy, who'd never shown any interest in so much as microwaving leftovers.

"Since your grandmama told me to watch her soup," he said. "She told me to tell you to come to the trailer when you got here. She's waiting for you."

"Why? What's wrong?"

Flavio shrugged. "None of my business."

Elpidia walked out the back door of the kitchen. Her grandmother's trailer was sitting where it always was, on the other side of the cement lot behind the cantina. It was a double-wide, and Elpidia had even had her own room when she came to live with her grandmother. She jogged across the lot and up the few steps to the screen door.

The first thing Elpidia saw when she entered the trailer was Abuela, sitting in her favorite armchair in the front room, apron and housecoat on, cane resting between her legs. Her eyes, as always, were hidden behind their dark shades, but Elpidia thought she looked upset.

"What's going on—"

It took a second for Elpidia to notice they weren't alone. A tall, slender woman walked out of the narrow hallway that led to the bedrooms. She smiled at Elpidia with a burst of emotion in her dark eyes.

It was Elpidia's mother. She was just standing there, like no time had passed since they were last together.

It felt like a dream. Her mother didn't look anything like she had the last time Elpidia saw her, wearing handcuffs and being put into one of the sheriff's cars. Elpidia had refused to go to her trial. Not even Abuela could convince her.

She remembered seeing her mother's face for the last time through the window of that car. She looked so sick. Her skin was gray, and her face was thin and sunken in her cheeks. Her teeth looked small and stained and gross. Her eyes looked like they were full of milk.

That wasn't the woman standing in front of Elpidia now. Her mother looked beautiful. Her hair was shiny and curly. Her skin almost looked like gold in the light. The skin on her face didn't look like it was stretched over her bones. Her clothes were clean, and she smelled like perfume. And her smile was bright and white.

"Hello, baby girl," her mother greeted Elpidia, looking like she was about to cry.

"You're out," Elpidia said, her voice flat.

"I am. For good, I hope."

Seeing her mother again was like seeing a ghost, and not because Elpidia had considered her dead or gone forever just because she was in jail.

No, it was seeing her mother look healthy and all the way awake with those clear, bright eyes.

That was the version of her mother that Elpidia thought was gone forever.

"You look . . . good," Elpidia said carefully.

"I feel good. I'm not . . ."

The wide smile her mother had been wearing faltered.

"I was going to say I'm not sick anymore, but that's not true. I'll always be sick, in a way. But I'm not drinking or taking anything anymore. I'm clean."

Elpidia suddenly saw an image of her dad flash inside her head.

"What about Papi?" she asked.

Her mother's smile disappeared entirely.

"He's still inside. He's . . . he's still not doing well, baby. He tried. We both said we'd try to get better when we first got locked down. He couldn't do it. It's hard. It's been hard for me, staying clean."

"How long?" Elpidia asked.

"For me? Eight months and seven days."

"No, I mean how long have you been out?"

"Oh. Three months."

Elpidia frowned, taking a step back away from her.

"And you're just coming home now?"

"That was my doing, mija," Abuela said quickly. "I didn't want your mother seeing you again until I knew . . . until I was sure she was better. That she was *really* better."

"And I needed time, baby," her mom added. "I needed some time to start getting my life back together. I had to find a job and a place to live. I have both now. Up north, in Anaheim. It's by Disneyland!"

Elpidia didn't understand. "Why so far up north?"

Her mom sighed heavily. Whatever she was about to say next was hard for her, it looked like.

"I can't come back here, Ellie. I mean, I can't . . . live here anymore. In the Estates."

Elpidia looked at her grandmother, hoping for some kind of explanation.

Abuela just tapped the end of her cane against the floor and then pointed it at Elpidia's mother as if telling Elpidia to talk to her directly.

"Why not?" Elpidia asked her mother.

"The same reason I can't be with your papi anymore, baby, even if he does get clean and get out. We . . . we're bad for each other. We still love each other. I'll always love your father. But we . . . we bring out that thing in each other that wants to drink and do all the other things that got us here. Even when we don't mean to. Even when we try not to. This place is bad for me in the same way."

Elpidia felt something hard and painful in her throat.

"Does that mean you don't want to be around me, either?"

"No!" her mother said, concern filling her face. "No, not at all! You're the person I care about seeing the most!"

She took two steps toward Elpidia, who didn't back away. Her mother slowly sank to her knees and reached out to place her hand on Elpidia's shoulders.

"I want you to come with me, baby," she said. "I want us to start over. I want to make everything up to you."

"Mija," her grandmother finally spoke up, talking to Elpidia, "no one is going to make you do anything. I still have custody of you. You can keep living with me if you want. I love having you here, always. But I believe your mamá. She's done the work. She wants to raise you again, and I think she can do that. I'll still be here, for both of you. We'll all still be here. But the choice is yours."

Elpidia had to swallow to get rid of what felt like the biggest lump in her throat. There was too much in her head, too many different thoughts and feelings and questions.

"What about the cantina?" she asked her grandmother. "What . . . what you were talking about at the motel."

"Don't worry about any of that," Abuela instructed her. "You have to do what's right for you. Not what's right for me or anybody else. The cantina will be fine."

It helped to hear that, but it was still hard. As much as she loved working in the kitchen with her grandmother, and as much as she knew Abuela loved the cantina, Elpidia still didn't want her life to be here in the Estates forever. If she took over the cantina someday, she knew she'd never leave.

"You don't have to decide right now," Elpidia's mother

added quickly. "Take all the time you need, okay? In the meantime, I can visit every weekend, if you want."

Elpidia just nodded. She didn't know what else to say. Her brain felt like it was on fire.

"Can I have a hug, Ellie?" her mom asked.

Elpidia looked up at her. Even though she was smiling, her mom looked so sad and desperate. Elpidia could almost see her remembering every bad thing she'd done to her before their house burned down.

Elpidia nodded.

Her mom took two steps forward and dropped to her knees, slipping her arms around Elpidia and gently pulling her close.

Elpidia held back at first, barely hugging her. But then she smelled her. It smelled like her mom, her mom *before* she smelled from alcohol and not showering. Elpidia felt like a little kid again. She hugged her mother back, tightly, and a second later they were both crying into each other's shirts.

It felt awful and good at the same time, and in that moment Elpidia never wanted it to end.

21

"If the inside of the pan catches on fire,
you have to have something to
smother it out. Air feeds fire the same
way it feeds us."
—ABUELA

Stan thought he was going to choke to death on the dust
that kept pouring through the open windows of the old
car. Elpidia told him he'd get used to it, and that the heat
when the windows were rolled down was worse, but Stan
wasn't sure he believed her.

She'd been really mad at him when he finally turned
up at the cantina after her having not seen him for days. At
least, she'd been mad for a minute. After that Elpidia was
just worried about him and wanted to know if he was okay
and what had happened. He told her he'd needed some

time to heal up, and that he'd had to sneak back home to see his mom and let her know he was okay. He told her about the fight with Los Cocos and about his father.

"You should call the sheriff," Elpidia said when Stan showed her what was left of the bruise on his chest, which was now sickly shades of yellow and green.

"My mom's called him before," Stan told her. "She never wants to send him to jail, though, and unless she presses charges, the sheriff says he can't do anything. Besides, all they'd do is take me away and put me in a home somewhere. I don't want that."

Elpidia didn't have any answers for that. She was just mad. Stan liked how much she seemed to care, anyway.

She couldn't believe what happened with Los Cocos and Charlie.

"I'm worried about what else they're going to do," Stan said.

"Charlie can handle it," Elpidia assured him.

Elpidia's tío Raymond was driving them out to Charlie's for their training session. Stan had told his mom he was going to stay the night at Elpidia's trailer, and that she should take the truck and go see her sister in El Centro for a few days. He figured they both needed a break from their house and his father, especially after his last blowup the week before.

"Raymundo Rides," he announced grandly to them like Stan and Elpidia were supposed to be impressed. "That's going to be the name of my company."

He'd been telling them, whether or not they wanted to hear it, about his plans to open his own chauffeuring business.

"I don't wanna just drive Abuela around forever, you know. I've been doing Uber and Lyft on the side. I'm saving my money. I'll start with one really nice car, and then before you know it—boom!—I'll have a whole fleet of, like, Chevy Suburbans."

Elpidia rolled her eyes and grinned at Stan, like her eyes were making a joke about her uncle and his big plans. After that Raymond put earbuds in his ears and started playing music on his iPhone, and Elpidia told Stan he couldn't hear them anymore.

"Listen," she said, getting serious. "I need to tell you about some stuff, too."

Elpidia told him about her mother coming back and surprising her, and everything she'd said to Elpidia about what happened and what she wanted to do from here.

Stan was happy for Elpidia until she got to the part about her mom wanting Elpidia to come live with her up north in Anaheim, near Disneyland.

"That's, like, three hours away," Stan said, regretting

right away that it was the first thing he'd said to her after she told him all that.

"I'm sorry. I'm really happy for you, and for your mom. I'm glad she's out and that she's better now."

"It's not like we couldn't still be friends or like we wouldn't talk," Elpidia told him. "I'd call. And there's email and stuff."

"I don't even have a phone that can do email. So, you think you're going to do it, then?"

Elpidia shrugged. "I don't know. Abuela believes she's changed. And Abuela is hard to convince."

"I just don't . . . I don't know what I'm gonna do with you gone."

"You'll keep training with Charlie. You'll make new friends."

"No, I won't. You know I won't."

"You *could*."

"Maybe I *should* just join Los Cocos. At least then I wouldn't be alone, and no one would mess with me."

Elpidia frowned. "You know better than that. Besides, what about our bookstore and kitchen?"

"That's not gonna happen and you know it. I know you were just being nice, talking about all that stuff. You want to do your food truck. You don't want to be stuck in some bookstore with me."

"I wasn't being nice! I think it's a great idea! And the truck . . . I still want to cook, but the truck was always about getting out of here more than anything. If I can get out of here anyway, the truck doesn't seem so important anymore, I guess."

"That's my point. Once you're out of here . . . why would anyone wanna come back?"

"I'll still want to see Abuela and my uncles and you."

"For a while, maybe."

Elpidia started to get mad.

"Look, don't use me as an excuse to stay here forever and mess up your whole life!"

Stan was about to say something back to her just as angry, but he stopped.

"Do you smell that?" Stan asked.

"What?" Elpidia asked, still thinking they were fighting.

It smelled kind of like someone grilling barbecue, only it didn't make Stan hungry. The dust wafting inside the car had started to turn into smoke.

It finally hit Elpidia, too.

"Something's burning," she said with her nose wrinkled.

Behind the wheel of the car, they heard Raymond curse as he stared out through the windshield.

There was fire all around one end of Charlie's

compound, where his little shack was. The house and the garage looked fine, but smoke was billowing into the air above them and getting blown by the wind across the desert, past Charlie's barbed-wire fence posts.

"Stop the car! Stop the car!" Elpidia yelled at her uncle once they were past the fence.

Raymond skidded the car across the sand when he hit the brakes, and then he turned off the engine.

"You two stay in here—oh, hey, come on, y'all! Come back here!"

Stan and Elpidia didn't even pretend they were listening to him. They both pushed open the heavy doors of the old car and jumped out onto the sand, running across Charlie's land past the house and the open garage so they could see the source of the fire.

It was the shack, or at least it used to be.

There was barely anything left of it. The whole thing had collapsed in on itself, just like Elpidia's old house.

They couldn't see anything beneath all the rubble.

"Was he in there?" Stan asked frantically.

"I don't know!" Elpidia yelled. "Charlie?!"

They both started looking around and calling his name, but there was no answer.

It was Elpidia who ran to check the house first. Stan followed her. They'd never actually been inside Charlie's house before. When they ran through the front door, they found there wasn't much to see. A little spare-looking cot he slept on. A space with a mini-refrigerator and a plastic gallon jug of water bolted to the wall with a rubber tub under it he must've used to wash up.

The only thing that jumped out at them about the space at all was a little display box that hung above the bed. It was filled with military medals of various shapes and with different colored ribbons attached to them. Charlie must have received them when he was a soldier.

His medals were there, but there was no Charlie.

They ran back outside and checked the garage, but he wasn't there, either.

By the time they'd finished in there, they came back out to find Raymond kneeling by the fiery remains of the shack.

"Tío!" Elpidia called to him. "We can't find Charlie! He isn't—"

"He's here," Raymond said, his voice practically shaking apart from what he was seeing. "Don't come over here! I mean it! Stay there!"

Stan and Elpidia looked at each other. They both knew what Raymond meant without either of them having to say it.

Charlie was dead. He was burned up in the rubble.

Neither of them could believe it.

Stan wasn't sure which one of them melted down first, but the next thing he knew they were hugging each other and crying and falling to their knees there in the sand.

Tío Raymond called emergency services, and they said they were sending the police and the fire department. Sheriff McCann was the first one to arrive. The little fire truck, not even one of the big shining red engines like you see in the cities, didn't show up until almost forty minutes later. By the time the firefighters made it to Charlie's, there was no fire left to fight. The desert had put it out for them. All the plants near the old shack had burned away to nothing, and there wasn't anything else past them for the fire to spread to, just sand and rocks.

"It's hard to tell," one of the firefighters said to the sheriff, "but I'd say his cook went wrong and the whole thing blew."

It took them less than ten minutes to decide Charlie's death was an accident. The rest of what they talked about was how they were going to clean up the whole mess.

That was it. Charlie was dead, and all they were worried about was the mess the fire had left behind.

Stan sat with Elpidia in the back seat of Abuela's car with the doors open. They were both holding the scorpion pendants Charlie had made them to show they were trained and to remind them of him, their teacher.

Stan clenched his fist around his pendant so hard, his knuckles were white.

Tío Raymond was still outside, talking to the sheriff's deputies.

"Mezco did this," Stan said, angrily, streaks of tears drying on his face in the heat. "I know he did."

"They said it was an accident," Elpidia reminded him, her voice still shaking. "Whatever he was doing in that shack, it went wrong, and he blew himself up."

"No, he didn't!" Stan insisted. "He was too smart for that!"

"If he was really smart, he wouldn't have been doing what he was doing."

Stan was shocked. "How can you say that?"

"Because it's true, okay? My parents did the same thing! Charlie just wasn't as lucky."

Stan had forgotten about Elpidia's mom and dad. It must've been extra hard for her to see this. Stan felt bad enough that it cut through his anger and pain.

"I'm sorry," he said quietly. "I forgot."

"I loved him, too," Elpidia said.

"I still don't believe it," Stan said, more calmly this time. "You didn't see the way Mezco looked at him."

Elpidia sighed. She didn't say anymore. It was clear she

didn't want to keep arguing.

"I'm not going to let them get away with this," Stan whispered.

"Stan," Elpidia said seriously, staring at him hard. "Don't do anything stupid, okay? Promise me?"

He nodded, but she felt like he hadn't even heard what she said.

Raymond leaned inside the car to talk to them.

"There's nothing else we can do here, you guys. I should take you home."

Stan wanted to tell Raymond that as far as he was concerned, *this* was home, but he knew Elpidia's uncle wouldn't understand.

That's when he knew he'd lost two things that day. He'd lost Charlie and one of the only places he felt like he belonged.

Stan wanted to cry all over again, but he didn't. He focused on being mad at Mezco, instead.

Anger felt better than being sad.

22

"Don't fight because you're angry.
Fight because you have no other choice,
and if you're angry, use it like fuel.
Don't let the anger use you."
—*CHARLIE*

Stan felt like a zombie walking back inside his house.
Everything inside him just felt dead, except for the parts
that were mad. He wasn't crying because he didn't have
any tears left.

Out front, the truck was gone, which meant his mom
was still gone. He was glad about that. He didn't want
to see her right now. He didn't want to have to explain.
And he didn't want her to try to stop him from doing
what he needed to do. For the same reason, he'd had
Raymond drop him off back home instead of taking him
to Abuela's trailer with Elpidia.

Stan hefted the strap of the skinny bag that hung from his shoulder. Several of Charlie's treasured rattan sticks were inside. Normally, the sheriff had told him, he wouldn't let anyone take anything from a scene like back at Charlie's, but McCann knew Charlie had no family and everything there was probably going to end up in a dumpster before long. It hurt Stan to hear that. He planned to go back for Charlie's military medals and some other things, even if he had to sneak or break inside the house, but he'd wanted the sticks right away.

The first thing Stan heard when he went inside was his father snoring on the living room couch.

He thought he smelled gas. Sometimes when he was drunk, Stan's father would try to cook for himself, and he'd leave the stove on. More than once Stan had to open all the windows and go around with one of their cheap plastic oscillating fans to get all the gas out.

That night Stan didn't care. He hoped there was a gas leak, in fact, as long as his father was the only one home.

He went to his room and started digging through his closet. Stan pulled out the one hoodie he owned. The only time it ever got cold enough to wear a jacket in the Estates was late at night.

Stan put on the hoodie and zipped it up. He slung Charlie's stick bag across his back like it was Hawkeye's arrows. He had also brought in an old roll of gray duct tape from the garage. He peeled off a little bit of a strip and started wrapping the thick tape around his right hand, specifically his knuckles and the bottoms of his fingers. He wrapped layer after layer until it felt like armor covering his skin.

Stan made a fist and punched into his other hand with it. He liked how it felt. He knew it would hurt more and cause more damage if he landed a punch on someone else with his fist taped like that. And it would protect his hand.

That was everything, he thought. He was as ready as he was ever going to be.

Stan didn't usually like looking in the mirror. He didn't like seeing himself, how fat he was. Tonight he stopped to check himself out. He even pulled his hood up. Maybe it would make him look cool and tough.

It didn't. He still just looked like a fat kid playing dress-up or something.

Instead of making him feel bad, though, it actually helped Stan. This wasn't pretend. It didn't matter if he looked cool or tough. He wasn't a character in a story. In real life, the toughest people didn't look like superheroes.

He left the house quickly, full of nerves. It helped to walk fast, almost like it helped him feel calmer.

Stan thought he saw something moving in the brush out of the corner of his right eye. Before he could turn toward it or reach for the stick bag, that something ran out of the darkness of the desert and crashed into him like they were trying to knock Stan over.

Instead he grabbed on to whatever or whoever it was and held them still.

"Let go before I throat punch you!" Elpidia snapped at him.

He let her go.

"What are you doing here?" Stan hissed.

"You're going to find Mezco, aren't you? You said you wouldn't do anything stupid!"

"I have to! What if his gang goes after somebody else? Like my mom? Or you? Or Abuela and the cantina?"

"You can't stop them from doing anything! They'll kill you, you big dummy!"

"Then they'll kill me, and it'll be over! They won't hurt anybody else. I don't care anymore!"

"What are you even talking about? How can you say that?"

"What difference does it make what happens to me?"

"Just because Charlie's gone—"

"He's not the only one!" Stan yelled a lot louder than he meant to.

Elpidia looked like he'd just punched her with his taped fist. She went from shocked to mad.

"Don't make you doing this my fault!" she yelled back at him. "And don't act like you're doing it to protect me or anybody else! You just wanna fight somebody!"

Stan didn't say anything to that, mostly because he knew he couldn't.

Instead, he turned and walked away from her.

It didn't do any good, though. Elpidia ran right after him.

"Fine, if you're going, then I'm going with you," Elpidia insisted.

"You are *not*."

"You can't stop me! And if you try, you'll have to fight *me*. For real. Is that what you want?"

It wasn't, and Stan could see she meant it.

"Fine. Just . . . stay out of the way. And be ready to run when it's time."

Stan started walking faster and taking longer steps, moving ahead of her. His legs were longer than hers, and Elpidia had to run even faster than before to catch up.

After walking the width of Lakeshore Estates, they saw their second fire of the night off in the distance. There were actually a few of them, burning in the dark.

Los Cocos were having what looked like a heckuva party in the ruins of the old stone house. They'd lit a bunch of fires in old metal trash cans for light and heat.

There was music playing from an iPhone hooked to two big speakers on the steps of the chimney. They had coolers full of drinks. One of them was even grilling what smelled to Stan and Elpidia like carne asada over one of the trash can fires.

Stan and Elpidia stopped where all the Los Cocos' bikes were parked. None of the gang members or their girlfriends had seen the two of them yet.

"What is your plan?" Elpidia whispered to him "You gonna fight them all? Who do you think you are?"

"Not all of them," Stan corrected her. "Just Mezco."

"How does that work?"

"I'm gonna call him out. In front of everyone. I'm gonna embarrass him. He'll have to fight me one-on-one."

"How do you know he'll *have* to?"

"That's how it works!"

"Yeah, on TV! And what if they all jump on you, anyway?"

"Then like I said, that's when you run away."

"You're just saying that because I'm a girl. I know how to fight just as well as you."

"I'm saying that because you're half my size, and they probably have knives and guns and who knows what. So run!"

Stan didn't want to argue with her anymore. He started

walking toward the ruins.

After a few seconds, Elpidia followed.

They walked right past the remains of the house's north wall. The Los Cocos who first noticed them didn't say anything. They didn't really react at all. Stan thought maybe kids rolled in and out of these parties all the time, so it wasn't too weird seeing them.

Mezco was chilling in the middle of everything, reclining back on one of the bigger pieces of fallen rock.

"Big Boy!" he shouted at him merrily, like they were old friends. "And his ride-or-die chica!"

"I *really* hate that," Elpidia grumbled under her breath. "I am not your girlfriend."

"I know that, now shut up!" Stan whispered back at her.

He was trying to psych himself up.

"We just came from Charlie's place," Stan said.

"Oh yeah?" Mezco looked like he didn't know what Stan meant at first, then he said, "Yeah, we heard there was some noise out that way. Sheriff. Fire Department. What did our Carlito do now?"

There were some scattered laughs among the gang members.

Stan suddenly found he didn't need to hype himself up. Mezco playing dumb, the rest of them laughing after what had happened, made Stan mad, and the anger was all the hyping up he needed.

"You *know* what happened! You killed him!"

Everybody got quiet when he said that.

Everybody except Mezco.

He actually laughed at that.

"Is that what's up?" His laughter faded away suddenly, and the expression on his face turned serious and dark. "So, Charlie's cook hand finally got away from him, eh? That's why the fire truck. He exploded himself, didn't he?"

"Stop pretending you don't know what happened!"

Mezco stood up from his rock and walked over to Stan, standing with just a foot of space between them.

"What'd you come here for, Big Boy? What, you wanna scrap? You gonna fight all of Los Cocos by your lonesome? Or is your chica here your secret weapon?"

"I didn't come here to fight everybody," Stan said. "Just you."

He slapped Mezco across the face with his untaped hand. Stan wasn't trying to hurt him. He just wanted to embarrass him.

Mezco might have been embarrassed, but if he was, he hid it well behind an expression that looked more like he wanted to murder Stan next.

Beside him, Elpidia started whispering to herself over

and over, so low only he could hear, "This is so dumb, this is so dumb, this is *so dumb* . . ."

As big as Stan was for his age, Mezco was still more than a foot taller than him, and his muscles looked bulgier than they ever had before.

"All right, then," he said calmly. "Let's do this. Tell you what, street fighter, I'll even make it easier for you."

Mezco got down on his knees, making Stan taller than him.

There was more laughter from his crew.

"This isn't funny," Stan told him.

"No, it ain't," Mezco agreed.

His fist flew out of nowhere, popping Stan hard right in the teeth.

It stung, but the surprise was almost worse. It threw Stan off right away. He tasted blood in his mouth and didn't even know where exactly it was coming from. His teeth felt weird and wiggly, too.

Adding to it, as soon as Mezco hit him, everyone started cheering and hollering all around them like they were at a boxing match.

Stan quickly put his hands up, shaking off the shot he'd just taken.

"All right, bring it!" Mezco taunted him.

Stan tried throwing his taped fist right into the middle

of Mezco's face, but he ducked out of the way with ease. He moved really fast, a lot faster than Stan was used to.

When Mezco threw another punch, Stan tried blocking and counter-striking, but Mezco was so strong, Stan couldn't push his wrist away. The punch went right through Stan's block and hit him square in the chest where his bruise still was.

That hurt a lot, and Mezco knew it. He must've remembered the bruise was there.

Going high with strikes wasn't working, and Stan knew another couple of shots would take him down, if it even took that many shots.

Mezco was laughing and having a good time, but he was keeping his guard up high to protect his face.

Stan jerked to one side and kicked Mezco in the gut as hard as he could.

It surprised the gang leader, who doubled over onto the rocky ground with the wind knocked out of him.

Stan knew this was his chance. He practically fell on top of Mezco's exposed back, crushing Mezco's body to the stone floor of the house with all of his weight.

At the same time, Stan started throwing elbows and punches at the Los Cocos leader's bald head.

The crowd made up of Los Cocos and their girlfriends booed and cursed and hurled insults at Stan, but Stan didn't care. He felt like he could actually win this fight.

He felt that way right up until, with a savage growl, Mezco rolled over and swept Stan to the ground with his powerful arms.

In the next second, Mezco was on top of him, pinning Stan's arms with his knees, and Stan knew he was done for. Mezco was going to crush his head into the rocks that he could feel under the back of his skull. It would only take one punch to do it, too.

Mezco never got to throw that punch, though.

The same way she'd been when she ambushed Stan back outside his house, Elpidia flew over them in a blur. She jumped into Mezco like a missile with both feet first, and the soles of her sneakers slammed into the side of his head, bending his cheek all the way until it touched his shoulder. The force of it knocked him from on top of Stan and onto the ground, where Mezco rolled a few times before stopping.

He didn't get up.

The crowd fell dead silent.

"You okay?" Elpidia asked Stan, trying and failing to pull him up off the ground.

Stan was eventually able to stand on his own, even if he did lean on her once he was back on his feet.

They both stared across the ruins at where Mezco was crumpled up on his stomach. He still wasn't moving.

Then, slowly, he began pulling his arms up where they were lying limp at his sides. They heard him start coughing, and once he'd hacked up what sounded like his whole lung, Mezco began doing a slow push-up with his hands and arms.

Stan and Elpidia looked around at all the members of Los Cocos watching their leader and the two kids.

It was like they were just waiting for Mezco to give them the word to tear Stan and Elpidia apart.

"I told you to run," Stan whispered.

"I told you this was a stupid idea," she whispered back.

Mezco raised himself up to his hands and knees. He stayed that way for a minute, like he was trying to get his bearings.

Finally, he turned his body and sat down on the ground with his arms resting over his bent knees.

"Was I out?" he asked Stan and Elpidia.

The question surprised and confused Stan, but fortunately Elpidia nodded for both of them.

Mezco snorted, a crooked little smile forming in one corner of his bloodied lips.

"I guess that means you won, then," he said.

There were some murmurs and whispers from the crowd at that. They didn't sound happy.

Mezco looked around at his crew disapprovingly.

"I said they won!" he barked at them. "So what do you do for winners?"

Mezco started clapping his hands together.

Slowly, the other Los Cocos and their girlfriends joined in, until everyone was applauding Stan and Elpidia.

They looked at each other, and it was clear from their eyes neither of them could believe this was happening.

"All right, that's enough!" Mezco barked again, causing everyone to stop clapping.

To Stan and Elpidia he said, "Thanks for providing the evening's entertainment. I don't want to be a bad host, but I think it's time for y'all to go home."

"Absolutely," Elpidia said gratefully and without hesitation.

She pulled Stan along as best she could, but he only really started moving when he wanted to.

"Oye, white boy," Mezco said to Stan's back a moment later.

He and Elpidia turned around.

Elpidia felt tense and scared beside him.

"I didn't have anything to do with whatever happened to Charlie. He was a good cook and a good earner. I made good money with him. And you ain't worth smoking a fool over."

Mezco spit blood into the sand.

"You do got talent, though," he said with a toothy grin. His teeth were also stained red. "Your girl, too. This was a good scrap. Why don't we call it squashed between us? Because I feel like next time, one of us isn't walking away. You know?"

Stan nodded. It hurt to nod. Everything hurt.

But somehow he believed Mezco now. There was no reason for him to lie. There was no reason for him to do any of the things he did.

"Let's go," Elpidia urged him, tugging on his arm.

"That was like some WWE wrestling stuff you did back there," Stan said when they were halfway back to the bikes.

"Uncles," she explained simply.

Stan tried to laugh, but that hurt, too.

23

"WARNING:
HIGHLY FLAMMABLE MATERIAL"
—*GAS CAN LABEL*

He walked Elpidia home first. She told Stan she didn't need a bodyguard, but he said after the past couple of weeks, he felt like *he* did. That got her giggling.

"You always make me laugh," she said.

It was one of the best compliments he'd ever gotten.

As he walked home on his own, Stan finally unwrapped the duct tape from around his fist. The blood on it had darkened and started to crust up. Blood was gross, but Stan found it didn't bother him. He wasn't sure whether that was a good thing or not. It was the kind of thing he would've asked Charlie about.

Stan wasn't ready to think any more about that yet.

His father was right where Stan had left him, passed out on the couch in front of the television, surrounded by empty beer cans. He was still snoring like a car crash.

Stan stared at the back of his head for a minute. He didn't even know why he'd decided to come home. He needed to change his clothes and to take a bath—at least that's what he told Elpidia—but it was something more than that.

The house still smelled like gas. Stan walked into the kitchen to check the stove. He jiggled each knob just to make sure it was really turned off, and all of them were. Stan leaned in close and sniffed at the burners, but he didn't smell anything.

The kitchen didn't smell like gas at all, Stan finally noticed. It was just in the living room. He hadn't noticed before because he was in a hurry and his mind was on Mezco and the fight ahead.

He wandered back out into the living room, following the smell more closely with his nose. It led him to the couch.

It was Stan's father. *He* smelled like gas. It was coming from his hair and his clothes.

His clothes. They were all rumpled, and there were

black streaks on his work shirt and pants, like he'd been burning something.

Stan didn't really know why, but his head started buzzing. It was an annoying little thing at first, but it only took a few seconds for it to become loud and painful. He felt himself starting to sweat, too.

He wondered what was happening to him. He wondered what his father had been doing. The more he wondered, the worse he felt.

Then he looked down at his father's hand lying on the couch cushion. His hand was curled into a fist around something, and when Stan saw what that something was, his whole body went ice-cold. The buzzing in his head became like a scream.

His father was holding a belt. It wasn't the old man's belt, either. This belt had a big buckle attached to one end. It looked like it was broken, like the other end of the belt had snapped off it, or maybe been pulled so hard it broke.

The buckle had a scorpion perfectly preserved under glass on it.

It was Charlie's belt. There was no way there could be another one just like it.

Stan's father was holding Charlie's belt.

Stan couldn't think. He could barely breathe. He kept seeing Charlie's shack burned to nothing but a blackened pile of sticks, knowing Charlie was underneath all of that.

He slipped the strap of the stick bag from around his body without even really knowing what he was doing. Stan pulled two of the polished, matching rattan fighting sticks out of the bag and dropped the bag to the floor.

On the couch, his father shifted a bit in his sleep but didn't wake up.

Stan went from not breathing to breathing hard and heavy. He pressed the two sticks together and held them tightly in both of his fists.

This time when he stared at the back of his father's head, he saw a target.

Stan swung both sticks as hard as he could into the side of his father's skull. They smashed against his ear, splitting the skin there.

Stan saw his father's eyes snap open and heard a choked scream come out of his mouth. The old man rolled off the couch and fell to his knees on the floor, his face pressed into the carpet.

The blow actually seemed to wake him up. Stan's father was groaning and whining and grabbing at his bleeding ear.

"What did you do?!" Stan screamed at him through the tears and snot he hadn't even noticed filling his eyes and nose.

He walked around the couch to stand over his father,

still holding the fighting sticks, ready to swing again.

"Wha . . . what're you talkin' about . . . ? What happened . . . ?"

Stan's father shook his head slowly as if he were trying to clear it. He looked up with bleary eyes at Stan.

The clouds in his eyes were slowly replaced by rage.

"You little pig . . ."

He tried to push himself up off the carpet, so Stan hit him with the sticks again, across the back of his neck. He didn't stop, either. Stan brought the sticks down across his father's head and spine again and again, until his father curled into a ball there on the floor, trying to protect himself from the blows.

He almost sounded like he was crying now.

"Tell me what you did to Charlie!" Stan demanded, screaming so loud his lungs and throat hurt. "Tell me right now!"

"I didn't mean to!" his father whined.

Stan stopped hitting him. Both of his arms stung from how hard and how much he'd been swinging.

He waited, trying to catch his breath.

His father was crying now. Stan had never seen that before. He still sounded drunk. Stan didn't know if he was crying because of the beating Stan was giving him, or because he was remembering what happened with Charlie.

"I found his number on your mom's phone," he

mumbled, still sobbing, holding his arms over his face and head. "I went out there to tell him to leave her alone. When he turned away from me, I grabbed him by the belt and I picked up a rock and hit him in the head with it. He . . . he didn't get up. I panicked. I started the fire to hide what I did. It was an accident!"

Stan was shaking by the time his father finished. The sad, weeping man at his feet destroyed everything—everything he even got close to. Stan had always known that deep down, but this was another level. Stan felt sick. He wanted to scream more, and he wanted to throw up all at the same time.

His father uncovered his face and slowly got back onto his hands and knees. He started trying to push himself up from the carpet again to stand.

The next thing Stan knew, he was on top of his father's back, wrapping his arms around his neck and pressing the fighting sticks into his throat. It was a choke hold Charlie had shown him, the last-resort choke hold he was only supposed to use if his life was in danger.

Stan did his best to wrap his legs around his father's body so that he was clinging to the old man as hard and as close as possible. He was too heavy for his father to shake off. He couldn't stand and he couldn't get any kind of grip good enough to pull Stan off him. Maybe if his father had been sober.

Stan could feel his father's body getting tense and tight. He saw the man's already-red face getting even darker. Stan knew he couldn't breathe. He knew what happened if he kept choking him, too.

"Son . . . please . . . *son* . . ."

His father could barely get the words out.

It didn't make Stan stop. Hearing him call Stan his son *now*, in this moment, only made Stan angrier.

Another voice, inside Stan, was telling him not to do this, however. That voice sounded more like Charlie's than Stan's.

He deserves this, Stan thought.

But you don't, that voice answered him. *You'll never be able to take this back. It will ruin you. And whatever happens to him, he'll win because he'll make the rest of your life as bad as his.*

Stan could feel his father's body starting to relax, which meant he was passing out.

And if he passed out, only one thing came next if Stan kept choking him . . .

Stan let go, releasing his grip on the sticks and rolling off the old man's back.

He crawled across the floor and turned to sit against the wall. Stan tossed away the sticks he was holding. He was so out of breath from the strain of holding the choke, it was like someone had been choking him.

His father wasn't moving. It didn't even look like he was breathing.

"Dad?" Stan said, starting to feel panic rising through his body. "Dad, are you okay?"

There was no answer. There was nothing from the old man. Not the barest twitch.

With trembling hands, Stan reached across the carpet and picked up one of the rattan sticks from the spot it had landed when he'd tossed it.

Sliding forward onto his knees, Stan carefully poked his father's body in the side with the other end of the stick.

"Dad?!" he practically yelled.

All of a sudden his father came to life, sucking in a deep, awful-sounding breath of air, as if someone had been holding him underwater and he'd just broken above the surface.

Stan collapsed back against the wall. He'd never felt more relieved or more terrified in his whole life.

Even though he was alive, Stan could see the old man was in bad shape. He was coughing as much as he was breathing and still not moving much.

Stan noticed that the coughing was starting to bring up blood.

He went to the phone and dialed 9-1-1.

"Hello," he said to the operator who answered. "I need an ambulance, please. And . . . and the police, probably."

24

"You can run away from a fight if you
need to. There's nothing wrong with that,
no matter what people tell you. But you
can't run away from all the fights.
I wish we could."
—*CHARLIE*

Elpidia should have been exhausted, but she felt too wired from all the excitement and adrenaline of the evening to sleep. She still couldn't believe she and Stan had fought an actual gang leader and not only lived, but they actually kind of won? At least she hoped Mezco was a man of his word, and that whatever beef there'd been between him and Stan really was squashed.

She was sitting in the middle of her bed in the giant oversize T-shirt she always slept in, with a cartoon cat on it. The window next to the bed was open, and Elpidia was enjoying the breeze that only came late at night.

She'd placed her scorpion pendant on the window-sill. It was hard to look at it, not just because she missed Charlie, but because it also made her feel angry. She hadn't wanted to talk about it with Stan because he was so upset and she knew he loved Charlie so much, but she was mad at Charlie. She was mad at him for cooking that poison and selling it to Mezco's gang.

She would never understand why anyone got involved with drugs. All it did was eat you alive. She'd watched it with both of her parents, and in the end it burned Charlie up.

Elpidia knew he was good. He had a good heart. Her mom and dad had good hearts, too. That's what was so horrible. Your heart was the first thing those drugs took away.

She was writing in her recipe notebook when Stan's face popped up above the windowsill and scared her half to death.

Elpidia whacked him with the notebook.

"Dude!"

"Sorry, I didn't mean to scare you."

"What're you doing here? I thought you needed to go back home?"

"I did," he told her. "I couldn't . . . I couldn't stay there, though."

Elpidia nodded slowly as she really looked at him. The expression on his face was hard to read. She couldn't tell if he was upset or sad or happy to see her, or all those things at the same time.

"You can stay here," she said. "You're always welcome."

"Thanks. Hey, I know it's weird to ask right now, but could you maybe make me something to eat?"

"Uh, yeah, I guess. Meet me around front, okay?"

Elpidia snuck into the living room of the trailer, not wanting to wake Abuela, who'd already gone to bed.

Abuela kept her big key ring with all the keys to the cantina by the door. Elpidia picked it up as quietly as possible before she unlocked the trailer door and stepped outside to meet Stan.

They crossed the lot, and Elpidia opened the cantina's kitchen door in the back and let them inside. She figured she could turn on just the lights in there and it wouldn't wake Abuela.

"What do you want?" she asked Stan. "To eat?"

"Whatever," he said. "Just something you like. One of your favorite dishes."

"There's some leftover ceviche in the fridge over here."

"That sounds great."

Elpidia nodded, still feeling confused about how he was acting, but she was still Abuela's granddaughter and feeding people came naturally to her.

She got the plastic container of ceviche out of the fridge and popped the lid open, grabbing a clean fork from where they kept all the silverware. She handed them both to Stan and then hopped up onto the kitchen counter to sit.

Stan ate fast and gratefully. It looked like every bite was changing his life for the better, in fact.

"This is *amazing*," Stan told her. "I never had food like this before."

"You should've grown up with my family. You still can, I guess."

"Yeah," Stan said without much feeling behind it.

He finished the ceviche and put the container and the fork down, wiping his mouth and chin on his hoodie.

"I should have told you to go," he said. "As soon as you told me about your mom coming back. I should have said you should go with her and get out of here, and you both should try to have a good life together. I'm sorry I made it all about me."

"It's . . . fine. You're acting really weird. What's wrong?"

Stan shook his head, but it seemed less like there wasn't anything wrong and more like he just didn't want to talk about whatever it was.

"I just needed to tell you that," he said. "I want you to be happy. And I know what you want more than anything is to get out of here. It's just hard because . . . you're the best friend I ever had."

Tears were starting to fill his eyes.

It broke Elpidia's heart to watch.

"I'm still your friend. And you're gonna get away from here too."

"I don't think so," Stan said so quietly she could barely hear him. "Not the way I wanted to, anyway."

Elpidia frowned. "What do you mean? What's going *on*, Stan?"

He ignored the question again.

"You know, the desert . . . my mom talks about how people moved out here to get away and be by themselves. But I think most people who came here and built all the houses . . . they thought the Estates were really gonna turn into something. You know? They thought this desert was going to become a big city someday, and they were getting in on it first. But that never happened."

Elpidia waited. She wasn't sure what Stan was getting at.

"This place was supposed to become something, and it didn't," he said. "I think the people here and their kids and their grandkids are the same way. They want to be something, but it never happens. I hope you can do better."

"Okay, seriously," Elpidia demanded. "What's going on with you? Tell me right now."

"I did something bad—" he started to say, but a loud noise and the flashing of bright red-and-blue lights through the windows of the cantina interrupted him.

The noise sounded like the siren of a police car to Elpidia.

She hopped down from the counter and went to the kitchen door, opening it to peer out into the cantina.

"It's the sheriff," Elpidia said, looking back at him.

"Stan, what happened?" she asked, suddenly very afraid for him.

"Every time I didn't hit him back, I felt like a loser," he said. "It was the worst feeling I ever felt. But you know what? It was better. It was the better thing to do. It's like Mezco said. He's not worth killing somebody."

Stan stuffed his hands inside the pockets of his hoodie and walked straight past her, out through the back door of the kitchen.

Still so confused, Elpidia ran after him.

The sheriff's car was just pulling around back when they all made it outside.

Abuela had come out of her trailer. She must've heard the siren and seen the lights, too. She was wearing a thick robe and leaning on her cane.

It was the first time Elpidia could remember seeing her without her dark glasses.

"Mija, come over here!" Abuela ordered her.

Elpidia didn't want to leave Stan, who was just standing there watching the sheriff climb out from behind the wheel of his car.

But she couldn't disobey her grandmother. She ran across the lot to stand by her side.

"What do you want, Sheriff?" Abuela asked him impatiently. "It's the middle of the night."

Sheriff McCann ignored her. He was looking directly at Stan.

"You know why I'm here?" he asked.

Stan nodded.

Elpidia thought he looked calm now. Somehow that was even scarier than the way he'd been acting just a few minutes ago.

"C'mon, then," the sheriff said to Stan. "Let's go. Your mom's worried sick about you. She was out all night looking for you even before we got the nine-one-one call."

That seemed to surprise Stan, but the look on his face was quickly replaced by something else, as if another, darker thought occurred to him.

"Is my . . ." Stan began, but his voice cracked, and he had to clear his throat. "Is my dad all right?"

"If you're lucky, they're patching up your old man right now and he'll be okay."

"Stan, what did you *do*?" Elpidia shouted angrily at him, but there were tears forming in her eyes.

Abuela held on to her shoulders tightly as they watched Sheriff McCann take out his handcuffs and cuff Stan's wrists behind his back.

"He's just a boy!" Abuela yelled at him. "You don't need to do all that!"

"Stay out of this, ma'am," the sheriff warned her, cinching each cuff tightly around Stan's wrists.

Abuela spat on the ground between them, whispering several curse words in Spanish that Elpidia had never heard her say before.

"Stan, I'm sorry!" Elpidia called out to him, not knowing what else to say.

She felt so powerless and helpless.

"It's okay," he said, sounding as calm as he looked.

He even tried to smile at her. It didn't quite come out right, but he tried.

It hurt so much as Elpidia watched the sheriff put Stan in the back seat of his car and shut the door on him.

"He'll be okay, mija," her grandmother tried to comfort her. "We'll help him as much as we can. We won't give up on him, okay?"

Elpidia nodded, but nothing felt okay.

Sheriff McCann drove off with the red-and-blue lights on top of his car blazing. Before he turned out of the lot, Elpidia saw Stan looking through the back window at them.

For just a second his eyes found hers, and she wished she'd said more.

She should have told him he was the best friend she'd ever had, too.

Epilogue

"It's only for right now."
—*UNKNOWN*

The place wasn't so bad, she supposed. At least, it didn't *look* so bad. Elpidia had only seen Stan's parent's old house from the outside, but the house he was staying in now was much nicer, cleaner, and bigger.

Of course, Stan wasn't the only kid living there. It was a home for a bunch of kids like him, who'd been taken from their parents for one terrible reason or another.

It was her first visit with Stan since he'd been placed here. She'd seen him for a minute in court when he had to appear before a judge, but they didn't really get to talk.

Abuela had kept her promise, though. She stayed in touch with Stan's mom and the caseworker they'd assigned him, so the family would know where he was and what was going on with him.

He'd finally gotten settled here a couple of weeks ago. Today was the first chance they'd had to drive up from the Estates.

They were waiting in a large living room near the front door to the place. After about ten minutes, Stan came down the stairs of the house to meet them. He looked happy. There was a big smile on his face. It helped Elpidia to see that after the way he'd looked when they parted.

The clothes they had him in, brown slacks and a plain blue shirt, were nice and new, but they didn't fit him at all. She knew that must bother him, but he didn't show it.

Stan received hugs from the rest of Elpidia's family, her mom and Abuela, and even Tío Raymond seemed happy to see him.

After they all said their hellos, Abuela tapped her cane and proclaimed they'd let Elpidia and him catch up alone, without the grown-ups butting in, and they left the room.

When they were gone, Stan just kind of stood there, looking at her. Elpidia was confused at first, even a little afraid, like maybe something was wrong. Maybe Stan had changed since she last saw him. Maybe he even felt differently about her now.

Then Elpidia realized what he wanted was to hug and he was afraid to make the first move.

Which meant Stan hadn't changed that much, after all.

Elpidia practically leapt forward and threw her arms around him. She couldn't quite make her hands touch because he was so much bigger than her and she wasn't tall for her age to begin with. She liked the way she felt kind of swallowed up by him, though. It made her feel safe.

For his part, Stan held on to her tightly and leaned his cheek against the top of her head. It felt like he didn't want to let go, like he was worried she'd just evaporate into thin air if he did.

Eventually they sat down at one of the tables that was kept out for visits.

"You doing okay?" she asked him.

Stan nodded. "Better than I thought I'd be doing. I miss . . . my mom. And, y'know, all you guys. But that's the only really bad part."

"What about the other kids here?"

He shrugged. "They're fine. They leave me alone."

"Because you're so big?"

Stan grinned. "I guess word got around I beat up a gang leader and my own father in the same night."

"I beat up the gang leader, technically," Elpidia reminded him.

Stan put a finger to his lips. "Shhhhhh. Don't tell anybody. Gotta protect my rep."

Elpidia giggled.

"Do you know how long you're going to be here?"

"No. But hopefully not forever. Mom was just here the other day. A woman from the court has to be with us when she visits me for now. It's annoying. But she _says_ . . . she left my dad. And that she's not going back."

"Do you believe her?"

"I want to. She says she's staying in a house kind of like this one, except it's for women who had to leave their homes because of people like my dad. She's looking for a better job and a place of her own to live."

"My mom's been through all of that," Elpidia offered. "Maybe she could help. Where is your mom looking?"

Stan smiled, looking down at the table.

"She asked me where I'd want to live," he said quietly, almost shyly. "I told her I heard Anaheim's nice. And I always wanted to go to Disneyland."

It took Elpidia a second to get why Stan had picked Anaheim. When it hit her, she smiled at him.

"Anaheim is really nice, yeah. We're liking it."

"So, maybe I'll see you there some time?"

"That'd be awesome," Elpidia agreed.

Her smile faded a little bit as she thought about something else.

"What about . . . your dad, though? It's cool if you don't wanna talk about it."

Stan shook his head. "It's fine. He's okay. As okay as he gets, I mean. He healed from that night. I'm glad for that, at least. They actually ended up arresting him after everything. They saw my bruises, and my mom . . . she finally stepped up and said something. So, they figured what I did was just me defending myself."

"That's good, Stan! That's all good stuff, right?"

"Yeah, I guess. Except . . . I wasn't just defending myself. You know that, right? I knew what I was doing."

Elpidia nodded slowly. "I know. But . . . that also means you made yourself stop, too. Think about *that*."

She thought hearing that actually seemed to make him feel a little better.

They spent the rest of the hour talking and sharing with each other what they'd been working on. Stan told her some of a new story he was writing about a prison floating around a planet in the future that gets blown out of orbit, and the prisoners and guards have to work together to save themselves. She showed him some new recipes she was working on, and some new ideas for both her food truck and their bookstore that would also be a restaurant.

Before they knew it, it was time to go. Visiting time was over.

"Oh, hey, we got you some stuff," Elpidia said, bringing up a plastic shopping bag she'd brought with her.

She handed it to Stan, who had a big grin on his face like it was Christmas morning.

In the bag there was a bunch of blank spiral notebooks and a box of pens.

"They're the kind you like, right?" Elpidia asked.

Stan nodded excitedly. "This is *perfect*! Thank you."

"You got a lot more stories to tell," she said.

Stan looked at her, and she could see he was feeling a lot and thinking about a lot inside that he wasn't saying.

"Yeah, I do," he agreed.

They hugged again, and Stan held on to her tightly and for a long time.

Elpidia could feel him starting to lose it a little and trying really hard not to.

"It's okay," she whispered. "I'll be back. And you'll be out of here soon. And we're gonna do everything we said we'd do. I promise."

She wasn't sure if he believed her, but it didn't matter either way. Elpidia was going to keep reminding him until things got better.

The words did seem to calm him down, though.

"I'll write you the rest of that story," he promised her, holding up his new notebooks.

After he was gone, Elpidia looked down at the table where they'd been sitting. Kids had graffitied all over it over the years, it looked like. There were gang signs and other things drawn in permanent marker or scratched into the wood.

One carving in particular caught her eye. Someone had gone over each letter at least a dozen times with something like a knife or maybe the edge of a ruler.

The carving read: "It's only for right now."

Elpidia nodded. That's what she'd want to believe if she was in this place, too. But it was also true for a lot of things in life, she thought, especially when you're a kid.

At least, she hoped it was true.

"Mija," Abuela called to her, waiting near the front door of the house with Tío Raymond and Elpidia's mom. "Vamos."

Elpidia nodded at her grandmother and took one last look at the carving before walking away from the table.

Next time, she thought, *I'll get Mom and Abuela to bring Stan some clothes that'll actually fit him. He'll like that.*

You couldn't make everything better all at once, she'd learned, but there was a lot of little things you *could* do along the way.

Acknowledgments

I want to thank you, the reader of this book, for taking the time to travel with me through a deeply personal story. I grew up in a world like Stan and Elpidia's, and a lot of the things that happen to them happened to me and friends of mine. It was healing to finally write about all of that, and I hope you took something from it. I'd like to thank my wonderful agent, Becky LeJeune, who boarded this ship late, but who played an instant and vital role in helping steer it back on course. My editor, Ben Rosenthal, has remained a constant and unfailingly supportive collaborator throughout my journey writing books for kids. Julia Johnson, a topflight editorial assistant, has been thoroughly delightful and helped keep us all on the right track. I'd also like to thank Katherine Tegen for believing in me and my work. I'm honored to occupy a small corner of the house she built. My mother, Barbara Wallace, who raised me on her own in a desert much like the one described in this novel, did a much better job than the mother depicted in my story. She also helped me recall a million tiny details from our time there that added to the world of the book. My wife, Nikki, is always my most valuable sounding board and the first line of defense between me and myself. I love her and am eternally grateful to and for her. Finally, my thanks to the rest of the crew at Katherine Tegen Books and HarperCollins Kids who contributed to this novel, including production editors Laura Harshberger and Jon Howard, managing editors Alexandra Rakaczki and Gwen Morton, designers Andrea Vandergrift and Amy Ryan, marketing manager Emily Mannon, Lauren Levite, production manager Kristen Eckhardt, and the School and Library team.